ELDRITCH TIDES

STORY CONCEPT BY
JASON MCKITTRICK

WRITTEN BY
JESSICA BURKE &
ANTHONY BURDGE

OTHER TITLES FROM MYTH INK BOOKS

These Dark Winged Ones
by Wilum Pugmire

Dark Tales from Elder Regions: New York
Edited by Anthony Burdge and Jessica Burke

The Friendly Horror & Other Weird Tales
by Anthony Burdge and Jessica Burke

"The Friendly Horror" audiobook,
read by Mars Homeworld

Tails from the Other Side: Pets & the Paranormal
Anthony Burdge, Jessica Burke,
and Christopher Mancuso

Forgotten Leaves: Essays from a Smial
Edited by Anthony Burdge and Jessica Burke

The Mythological Dimensions of Neil Gaiman
Edited by Anthony Burdge, Jessica Burke,
and Kristine Larsen

The Mythological Dimensions of Doctor Who
Edited by Anthony Burdge, Jessica Burke,
and Kristine Larsen

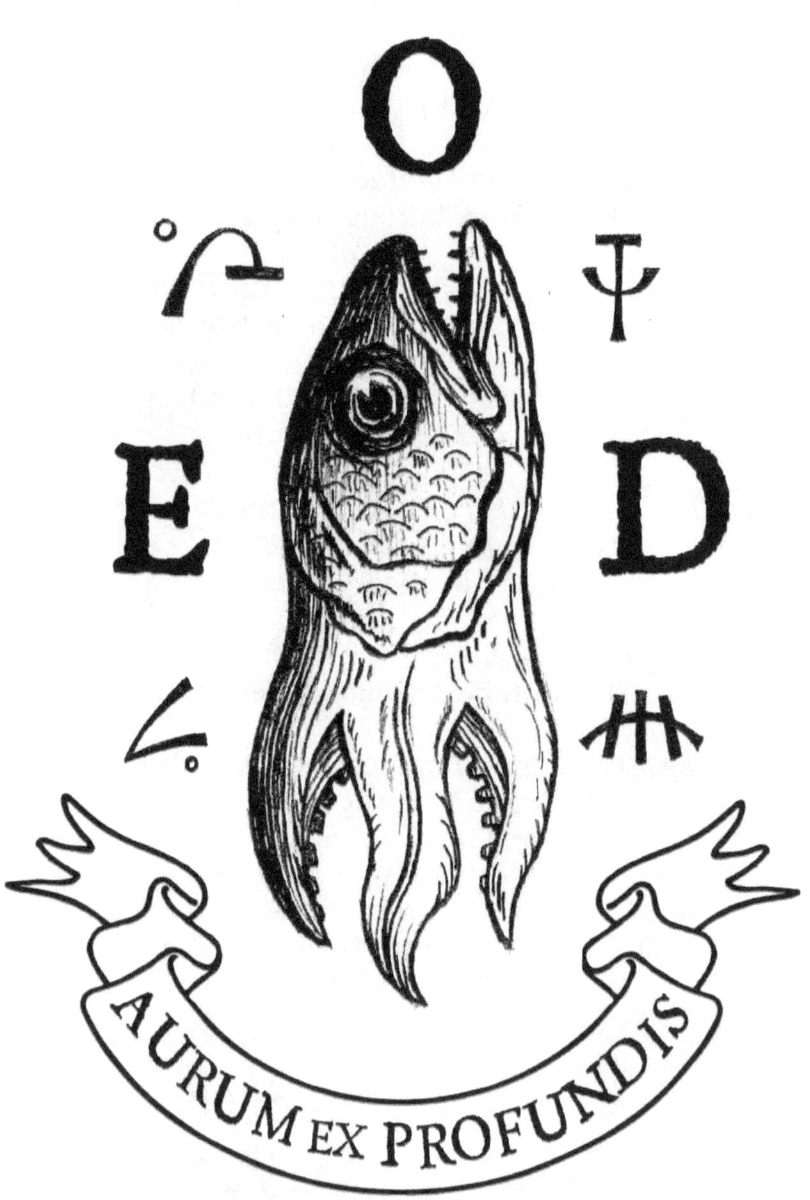
O
E
D
AURUM EX PROFUNDIS

To the next Generation:
Nora, Lily, Mia,
McKenzie, Maddie, Ellie, & Charlie
Weird is awesome.
Be Weird.

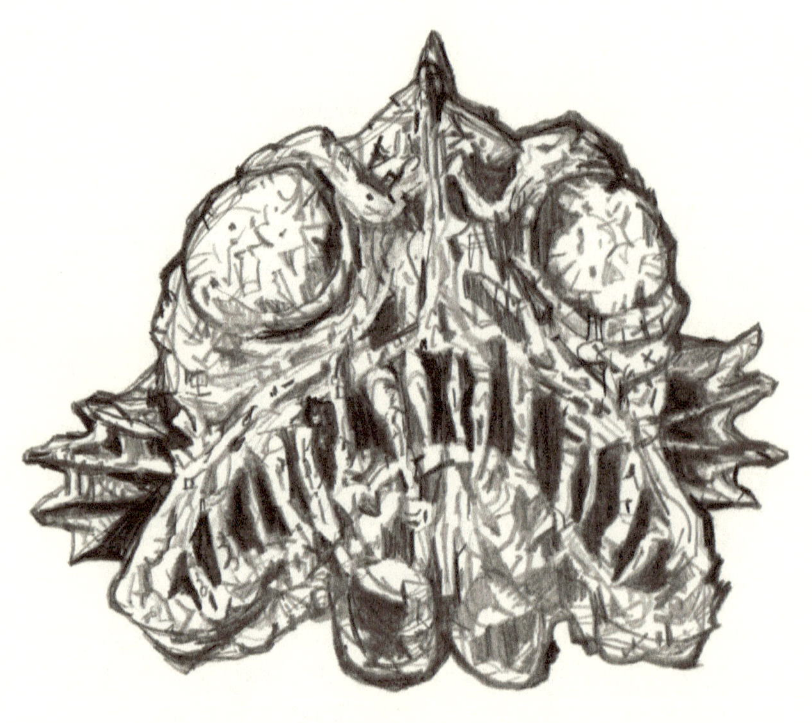

ACT I
JANUARY 22, 2005

WINTER STORM WARNING IN EFFECT

"Good afternoon, I'm Liz Cho, filling in for Sade Baderinwa. Here's a Winter Weather Advisory for today and many parts of the Tristate Area have already called a state of emergency. Get ready for a snuggle alert and what is being called Snowpocalypse because TONIGHT: snow, snow, and more snow. Lee Goldberg is with us for your storm track and forecast for this afternoon and tomorrow. Over to you Lee at the weather desk."

"Thanks Liz. I don't know about Snowpocalypse. I'm partial to Snowmageddon, but whatever you call it, this afternoon we're getting snow, which will be heavy at times. We'll get a few snow squalls and snow accumulations of 5 to 10 inches down at the Jersey Shore. Much of the Tristate is looking for a minimum double digit accumulation. Up in New England, they're getting slammed with a foot and a half as the baseline. Keep in mind, this is all on top of the 2 inches we've already got on the ground. *That* with the nice Arctic freeze dipping in from Quebec, expect highs in the lower 20s with a wind chill in the teens to single digits at best. The real feel outside, with the wind ripping off the water, is below zero. I expect the Winter Storm Warning to increase to a Blizzard Warning later tonight. For today, we're getting another 10 plus inches possible. Most areas of the Tristate, some areas of Port Jervis, Stamford, White Plains, down into Newark and Piscataway, over to Staten Island, and dipping into Central Jersey: we're getting 3-4 inches *per hour* with double digit snowfall total accumulation. Areas to the south, Little Egg Harbor and Millville can expect a dusting, but there are pockets around Baltimore that have pretty substantial accumulation. This storm is a wait and see for many areas. But, there's a good chance we're looking at the upwards of 10 to 16 inches for coastal New Jersey throughout Ocean County.

"Also, keep in mind, anything on top of a hard freeze means the roads are already treacherous. New York and New Jersey already have issued statewide emergencies. Right now, it's windy with lows around 15. East winds 10 to 20 mph, but as the storm intensifies overnight, those winds will be increasing to 20 to 30 miles per hour northeast with gusts up to 40 miles per hour after midnight. Wind chills will be a bit better than earlier today, with a balmy 16 degrees. Stay tuned for storm updates. Keep the blankets and flashlights handy, because as the power lines freeze and as the winds pick up, we can expect massive outages. Stay tuned to WABC for the latest storm updates."

JEREMIAH & MJ

"Why can't I use my potion of fire resistance and keep warm with the fireball? MJ you suck as DM," Jeremiah's face contorted into a grimace and he grabbed another cheeto.

"Get your orange mitts off my character sheets Jer. I don't want orange grease-stains. I suck? How the fuck can you expect to keep warm via fireball?"

"You said I've got a negative adjustment for the cold. And it's dark. We know Sahuagin are dark seekers. I've got to see. I don't have good night vision—"

"For an elf? A dark elf? Seriously Jerry. I know it's been a while, but come on. This is the last campaign here. You keep putting me off. We finished *Sinister Secrets of Salt Marsh* back in the fall and you breezed through *Danger at Dunwater* Thanksgiving weekend, but you've dicked me around since. Can we please finish this campaign and then you can take over for DM a while? You did well last one and even listened when I told you *Dunwater* wasn't a hack and slash. So why the hell are you going tits up now? We've got all weekend. We aren't going anywhere and if we lose power, I brought my mom's oil lamp. It will be cool to play by firelight. You think your mom will have a problem with us using it down here or do we have to go upstairs?"

"Yeah, probably.... Curwen's tired. It's taken ages to get here and yeah, we're only on Level One. And I can't take the B.S. villagers any more. If I get one more accusation, I don't give a fuck if Dagon eats them all."

"Sekolah. The name of the Sahuagin god is Sekolah."

"Sekolah Dagon. Same diff. He who eats; it that is eaten. Right now, the Sahuagin treat Curwen far better than those Saltmarsh fuckers. So I don't care if any more are carted off and offered to whatshisname."

"Sekolah. Besides, what do you expect when you play a lawful evil magic user who happens to be a thief as well? The Sahuagin are manipulative. They'll tell you what*ever* to get you to do what they want. What do you expect from fish-people? How do you know you won't be on the sacrificial block? Curwen is slime and even the NPCs know it. My campaign, *Curwen.* When you do your own thing, you can pull in some of those Dagon references from your family tree." MJ scowled, blowing a fiery curl out of her gray eyes. She ducked behind the DM's wall and wished she hadn't agreed to have a Blizzard sleepover. She could practically look into her room from here. Here in Jeremiah's basement, here on Buchanan Street, MJ's house was maybe two yards away. If she ducked further down, she could just see out the basement window and catch sight of the casement to her own bedroom, on the first floor. Jeremiah's house was a grand, full two story, with a basement and attic, while MJ's was just another bungalow in Gilford Park. Her parents had the spacious top-of-the-house room that was originally an attic, but dad had renovated it into a grand master suite. MJ was on the ground floor, at the back of the house, and her room looked onto Jeremiah's basement, which he mostly used as another bedroom. This was their go-to place since MJ's house was so small.

"Curwen is cold." Jeremiah interrupted MJ's mental meanderings, crunching another cheeto before he loudly finished the last of his Mountain Dew, relishing the rumble as he sucked at the bottom of the cup with his straw. "And if he uses his potion of fire resistance then the fireball should keep him warm while getting rid of the nasty damp bits."

"We're only on Level One. Above water." The sound of dice as they rolled on the wooden tabletop. "Looky there. You suffer a negative one on constitution—" Another click, clack, roll. "The potion is successful but—" Click, clack, roll. "Your fireball ricochets off the opposite wall. Remember how smooth the stones are? Volcanic glass —"

"You just made that up!" A cheeto whizzed over MJ's head, landing on a pile of blankets and pillows on the couch against the far wall behind her. Part of the pile separated, hissing and yowling. "Fuck off Mr. Flibble. Go back upstairs. Stupid cat." He tossed another cheeto.

She laughed. "Volcanic glass. Sekolah helped them outfit the walls with volcanic glass. The fireball flies over your head, and burns through one set of double doors.... revealing a Sahuagin sleeping chamber!"

"HA! I knew it. Those fishy bastards are everywhere."

"You're lucky that was it. I told you before: there might be a Gelatinous Cube somewhere... maybe...."

"Gelatinous Cube? Why would one of those be here at the Sahuagin fortress?"

"Payback for that fucking Duck Bunny you had the gall to call up last time. *Curwen.* You fucking tried polymorphing your horse into a damned Duck Bunny just to see if you could."

"Well you wouldn't let me steal your NPC's pants, so I Duck Bunnied out of there." Another cheeto flew across the room. "Don't forget, oh Dungeon Mistress, the roll was successful. As was the Alter Size spell. You're still kicking yourself that Curwen had enough juice to pull off both spells. He had a bonus spell in that round, fair and fucking square."

Footsteps on the stairs interrupted any retort. Mrs. Allen trundled down, her short frame hiding beneath her usual chunky sweatsuit, dirty blonde ponytail bobbing with each heavy step. She carried a tray with two prodigious bowls. "Here's the last of the Maxfield's. Before we lose power, have at it. We're all out of Golden Kraken, Jeremiah. I know you like that, but here's some Crustacean Creamsickle, and the Mermaid Melon Meringue. Halfsies each."

"You know I don't like the Mermaid Melon, *Donna.*"

"Mom, if you please Jeremiah. You've been here since you were a munchkin. We're your parents. I've said it more times than I want to remember. Call me mom, k?" She brusquely plopped down the tray on the other end of the old dining room table the kids sat on opposite sides of, spilling some of the root-beer she had also included, thinking the kids could make floats while they quested through the fortress of the fish-people, or whatever campaign they were on today.

"And ice cream? Today? It's what 10 degrees outside?"

"Jeremiah, your mom is being nice. Don't be a dick." MJ wasn't sure why Jeremiah was so horrible to his mother. Ok adopted, but still. She was bringing them fucking ice cream and letting her stay over until mom and dad got off their shifts, which wouldn't be for some time since hello Snowpocalypse. So why was her bestie such an asshole to his parents?

"Thank you MJ, but you know Jeremiah. Nothing I can do about that. Besides, this came for you yesterday. Dad got it confused with his stuff. Please don't let it be another stamp collecting gimmick. I don't want to have to cancel another subscription, Jeremiah." Mrs. Allen handed her adopted son a bulky, oil-stained, manilla envelope she had stuck under her arm.

"What the fuck, Donna? Marvin opened it. Can't he see my name there! Is this what happens when you get old? You can't read any more?" Jeremiah ripped the bundle from the woman's hand and made a weird clucking sound with his tongue as he took note of the torn top. His name was clear: Jeremiah Allen D'Bourget. But there was a red slash through the D'Bourget. The top corner, partly intact, had an oblong shape that looked like a half a bullet with a squiggle extending out of it with an Arkham, Massachusetts address. "These are from the archives at Orne. How could Marvin confuse this with anything of his? He's a fucking EMT, *Donna*. What would an EMT do with anything from the Orne archives?"

"You have no idea what your father does in his spare time. Besides, when he gets home, we're going to have a chat about this whole Donna-Marvin thing, ok Jeremiah? You want to take on your family name. Fine. You started this project at school. A fine thing for a kid in intermediate school. Research your roots. Family tree, whatever. But, this is going too far, young man. Play your board games—"

"AD&D is not a fucking board game, *Donna*."

"Play your whatever the fuck game. Eat whatever fucking ice cream you want. Play in the snow. Throw cheese doodles wherever— but when your father gets home, we're done with this attitude. Otherwise, no more packages from Ome."

"Orne. It's the *Orne* Archives at Miskatonic."

Jeremiah hugged the package to his chest like it was a baby. His green eyes were so bright they looked feverish. Mrs. Allen wondered if her adopted son had a cold or mental problems. She wanted to reach across and feel his forehead, but the phone rang upstairs and she decided against it. Shaking her head, she hurried upstairs, hoping her husband would remember after the ceremony to gather some of the snow for her. He didn't think it was a big deal, but it would be charged, the moon would be full, and it would hold the memory of the deed, the saltes. She would bottle it and use the spiked liquid for ages. It would be good to the last drop and she did give him a half gallon fucking jar to fill. She just wanted pristine snow and nothing contaminated with blood or ichor.

"So what's the deal with your mom?" MJ covered her notes,

scooted her chair over and stretched across the table to snag a bowl of Maxfield's bliss before it melted completely. "And yours? If I talked to my mom like that, I'd get a backhand. What's your problem, Jer?"

"She's not my fucking mother for one. Two, she smells. Three Marvin is a stupid name and four fuck you. Want to go home? Climb out the window like you used to when you were eight. Your room is right there." Jeremiah pointed over his head, to the window MJ had been looking at. "Besides, don't you want to hear what I got from Miskatonic? I wrote to the head librarian. I addressed the letter to Dr. Armitage, but I know he's long gone. I thought it was funny. I needed any information they had about my family."

"Why would they have it? Didn't you say your family was from France? And wasn't there someone who lived in Monmouth county? Why not write to the county records office there? Why up in Arkham?" MJ sucked on her spoon, washing down the Mermaid Melon with a sip of root-beer, not sure the two flavors really complemented each other.

"I already got the info I needed from Monmouth County. I needed the other stuff from Orne. They would have records, if any existed, of any alchemical past in my family and I wanted verification of any relation to the Curwens."

As MJ finished her ice cream, Jeremiah poured over the contents of the envelope. Not much, except several typed pages, a few xeroxes –photos, some with old writing that looked like calligraphy, maybe a birth certificate, and old newspaper clipping. Then she saw that the typed pages were double sided and single spaced. There was more there than she thought.

"This is awesome, MJ! This is exactly what I needed. I was right! My biological family name *is* Curwen!"

"Your player? Don't tell me you're a lawful evil dark elf too–"

"Shut up. Jealous much. I already told you. In school, for the project, I found out that a distant relation is one Marquis Antoine D'Bourget, who was exiled from France in 1780. It was soon to be Revolution time there and when I did some of my own research, I came up with another possible reason why he left. There was another wave of witch hunts, even in the midst of the Enlightenment. Louis XIV was an imbecile. As if there weren't enough problems, even before heads started rolling a few years later? But, I've always suspected the Marquis left because he might have been accused–"

"Of using magic? This isn't D&D, Jer."

"Alchemy, sorcery, these are all precursors to today's sciences. Chemistry, physics, metaphysics. But, maybe I'll find answers here. That's why I wrote Orne. The Marquis must've known the Frenchies were gearing up for Revolution especially after ours, so he got out while he could. He's the one that secretly lived in Monmouth County–"

"Why secret?"

"I don't know. He was French. The Brits were around. But, that was a school project. A primer. All I found out then was where the Marquis was from, where he went, and that maybe D'Bourget was involved with those Highwaymen, the Pine Barren Bandits. I was able to find out lots about them and I had suspicions that D'Bourget was involved with John Bacon and the Long Beach Island Massacre of 1782. That would explain why he lived in secret you smart-ass. My own research led me almost in a different direction to another family branch, the Curwens who were from Salem and Arkham. I've got to go through these—"

As he spoke, his eyes flashed and he bent over the pages, caressing them ever so slightly while scanning quickly as he spoke. MJ imagined she could see him ten years hence, studying as they both wanted to at Miskatonic. Jeremiah wanted to pursue a dual major, Occult Studies and Chemistry –which he said should have the old name: Alchemy. She wasn't sure, but leaned toward the Liberal Studies program, maybe history or something. But, he was the scholar, even now, weeks before their 13th birthday, which they didn't share exactly. She was two weeks older than he was, but often, since they became friends, they'd celebrate their birthdays together. She spent so much time here, at the Allens, she really didn't know why Jeremiah hated them so much. Mrs. Allen was so nice, especially to her and that old lady down on Minturn Road, who all the kids called the Minturn Witch. But she was just a nice old lady who collected Halloween decorations. Mrs. Allen always brought her hot soup on cold days, picked up her medications at the pharmacy, sometimes even spent whole afternoons reading to her. MJ knew Mrs. Allen had brought them the ice cream after she had just come back from having checked on the woman. Why was Jeremiah such an asshole?

"This supports my hunches. The Marquis was a Pine Barren Robber. At a quick glance, they say that shortly after arriving in New Jersey, the Marquis D'Bourget settled with one of the Marquis' own relations, one Jeremiah D'Bourget who happened to be a high ranking member of the Pine Bandits. It didn't last long, though, because he was hung."

"Who, the Marquis?"

"Jeremiah. It says," reading from the back of the first page. "By early 1782, the Marquis had a solid arrangement with Loyalist Captain and Pine Robber, John Bacon, a partnership once held by Jeremiah D'Bourget. Maybe the Marquis got his own cousin out of the way in order to get closer to Bacon?" Jeremiah laughed. He didn't even jump on his namesake.

MJ could see how small the print was. How could she have thought there wasn't much here? There was a fucking encyclopedia. She knew Jeremiah would be having wetdreams over this. Fuck the Sahuagin and Saltmarsh Villagers now. MJ eyeballed the melting bowl of Jeremiah's ice cream. She had just finished the last of hers and already had the ice cream shudders. That on top of the cold. The wind let out a high shriek, like the air being released from a balloon. She glanced out the window and saw how dark it had become, despite it being barely 3:30 in the afternoon.

"The Marquis was the one who instigated and organized Bacon and the Pine Robbers to slaughter thirty American sailors, plus assorted residents near Barnegat Lighthouse in the middle of the night. That was the Long Beach Island Massacre. Now, I see they're linking the Marquis to Joseph Curwen. Fuck yeah. I told you. I fucking TOLD you!"

Jeremiah was happier than a kid should be at reading this kind of thing. But, MJ supposed it was like a D&D campaign, realized. She thought she'd have the same frenetic look if she found out she had a real magic user in her family and if she had been named after someone cool like a highwayman.

Jeremiah continued.

"The Marquis' own dark magickal affairs can be tracked back, way before he left France. They say they sent me facsimiles of a few letters, dated 1769-1770 between the Marquis and Joseph Curwen. They both were in it MJ with their dark agenda." Jeremiah muttered, almost to himself. "He needed blood and he got it."

"What now?"

He ignored her and kept reading. "The Marquis D'Bourget soon became very acquainted with the Crane family in Elizabethtown, New Jersey through John Bacon who worked on their family farm in Manahawkin. The Crane family were ardent Patriots, and several were members of the Monmouth Militia. It is not said what the nature of their relationship was, but being involved with the Pine Barren Bandits, or Pine Robbers, it seems the Marquis was after occult documents, grimoires, spell books of all kinds. The Bandits were paid to hold up carriages crossing through the dense forest of the Pine Barrens. Somehow he knew who would be traveling the roads and targeted them for death, with their belongings brought to him. Convenient."

He laughed. The hollow sound seemed to merge with the wind screeching outside. MJ felt more than uncomfortable as she sipped her root-beer.

Jeremiah kept reading as though he was in the room by himself. "In this affair he shared with select members of the Crane family, who had a darker side to them, and the librarian notes that perhaps this was one inspiration for Washington Irving's own references to the occult in *The Legend of Sleepy Hollow*. There are even letters between the Marquis and Stephen Crane! But the librarian said she couldn't send copies of everything. She said she gave me a synopsis of stuff, but I should go see the collection for myself. She said the letters between Crane and the Marquis take an entire box. Between those and the correspondence with Curwen? It's a whole shelf almost. She says there are arcane spells to help direct weather conditions and target homes, people and so on. They say the last dated reference was 1782. They included it in the copies." Jeremiah fished through the small stack of papers and held up one with a hastily drawn image of a tentacled fish-head. MJ thought it looked a bit like the half-bullet from the torn front of the envelope. "There is no reference to the Marquis beyond the 1782 date. It says local folklore and press at the time allege he disappeared. You think mom would want to visit the Orne in the Spring?"

"You mean Donna? The woman you basically told to fuck off? The smelly one who was nice enough to let me sleep over? The one who's upstairs now making a mammoth bowl of freezer stew so we don't freeze in 30 feet of snow? Really? Ya think she'd let you do that you disrespectful little Sahuagin-loving freak?"

515 pm	BLZD CONDITIONS SEASIDE HEIGHTS OCEAN COUNTY, NJ	39°56'54.1"N 74°04'18.5"W
1/22/05	BLOWING SNOW. REDUCED VISIBILITY. WND DMG.	EMERGENCY MNGR

DISPATCH: "Dispatch controller Anziz SHPD771 on duty."

DISPATCH: "Car Alpha Bravo 1366, are you receiving?"

AB1366: "Alpha Bravo 1366 receiving loud and clear Dispatch, PC Berkana on duty."

DISPATCH: "Receiving you 1366. What's your location?"

AB1366: "Just east of 35 dispatch. Corner of Harding."

DISPATCH: "You solo this evening Berkana?"

AB1366: "10-4 Dispatch. PC Ford's wife went into labor. He'll be at Community now.

DISPATCH: "Blizzard baby. You shouldn't be by yourself tonight Berkana. We've got a report of shots fired just north of Hiering Avenue. Just near the monolith. A possible drunk and disorderly. Use caution. There's a Storm Surge. Can you get down there?"

AB1366: "10-4 Dispatch. Hiering and Boulevard should still be clear. I was just down there 20 minutes ago."

THOMAS

Figures. My lot to get a drunk, shooting off tonight during a fucking storm on one of those damned monoliths, too. Will wonders never cease. I always wondered why those things were never torn down. You hear all about them in Mystic Isle. They have a few. Used for Nazi sub alerts or something for the War. I used to climb the one on South Captain Drive when I was a kid. Fucking asphalt went right around it like it wasn't there. As kids, we used to try scaling the wall, pretending like we were Bond, scaling the cliffs of St. Cyril's. I even made a rope ladder and tried to use it without realizing someone had to go up top and drop the fucker down before anyone could climb up.

Dad said I was a moron.

But, I always wondered about them. They looked so much older. Like they had been bunkers used during the Revolution. No one ever talks about the Seaside Heights Monoliths though. Fuckers are three times as big. The one by Hiering has to be thirty feet high if it's an inch. Back in the late 90s a bar down the block, Hooks, built a staircase up one side. They had some wet t-shirt contest or July 4th fireworks extravaganza or some such nonsense. They had to build some kind of fencing around it to keep their patrons from falling off. The fencing was taken down, but the staircase had been left. It had been driven into the masonry with iron. The City Council thought they could make an observation post or something to rook in the tourists. And they did. For a while. But, after a kid killed himself, jumped off what six, maybe seven years back? Stairs were fenced off. Every so often though, we get calls. Especially during a full moon. Fun. Climbing up top in this weather? Ice and wind. I'll be lucky I don't get blown off.

DONNA & MARVIN

"How do you know he'll be the one sent, Marv? There are a lot of cops. Why would they send him?"

"You have to have faith, Donna. Thomas is on duty. There aren't as many as you'd think in the Seaside Heights PD. Especially tonight. Who the fuck wants to work during a blizzard anyway?"

"You did."

"I'm special. Besides, the Marquis has us all meeting up top. We've prepared for this. We'll be rewarded."

"Don't forget to bring me the snow."

"How could I forget? You shoved a fucking half gallon ball jar in my kit bag. What did you think the guys at Community wouldn't see? Don't you think we have specimen bags in the back of the wagon? I'm an EMT not Joseph fucking Curwen. You're into the whole essential saltes thing and our wonderful progeny has been obsessed with finding out his parentage. I suppose you gave him the package?"

"Of course I did. We were told to. It's all moving according to schedule. Tante Asenath sends her love. She won't be joining you tonight. Her joints haven't been right and she'll be taking to the sea soon anyway, so her presence might be redundant. The Marquis never liked her. After all her Waite blood, she's a Maxfield, too. She was born to it like her old Aunt Julia, when the Marquis has to earn his transformation. Asenath, like Julia, is a niece of Old Obed, don't forget. "

"Yeah. Don't remind me. Keep clear of the Minturn Witch, would you? I don't care if she's Mother Hydra herself."

"Don't be crass. I get enough from Jeremiah. Do you forget, lover, that she's my aunt? So, that means, way back, I've got a bit of the Marshes in me too."

"Cousin like seventy-two times removed, Donna. Asenath McGovern is a creepy old hag and I don't know why you keep going back to her hovel."

"Misogynist much? Don't forget yourself, lover. I take enough shit, as I said, from the Prince and his fucking aristocratic grandfather or whatever the Marquis is to the little prick. I deal with his mouth and the insults and I can't do a damned thing. Yet. Asenath McGovern has always been like an Aunt to me. She was the one who kept me safe after my mother's coven was razed. You *know* that. She has always been kind to us both. She's got my interests in mind *and* an eye on the canals. She'll let me know if anything turns up. The Marquis is our leader, unless he's challenged. She may. But, she'd rather go out to sea. I can't deal with you now, so please.....You want me to come pick you up tonight?"

"No. The storm is too bad. I don't want you on the roads tonight. Hunker down. I'll be back home tomorrow tonight after everything is done."

"You won't be missed?"

"Why? My shift ended an hour ago. I'm not back on until the morning. I'm not coming home though until tomorrow. Thomas is on duty and I saw his Sarah in the ED before I clocked out. The kids are occupied? MJ?"

"Yeah. I brought them some Maxfield's a while ago. You finished the Golden Kraken, Marv. I wanted to give Jeremiah some. Maybe it would calm him down a bit."

"He's got a role to play before this is done. We can't have him swimming off to Y'ha-nthlei with old lady McGovern, can we? Just deal with him a little while longer. We'll be taken care of, ok?"

"Yeah babe. I'll see you tomorrow. Hugs and smoochies."

BLIZZARD MYSTERY ON THE MONOLITH

"Toni Yates reporting on the scene in Seaside Heights. It's bad enough we're in the middle of a winter storm that was upgraded to a blizzard last night, but now we've got what looks to be a murder scene at the Seaside Heights Monolith behind me. Neighbors awoke to over a foot of snow and a dune over 2 feet high at the base of the monolith. A dune covered in blood. Here's Hepzibah Lawson, the neighbor who first called police. What did you see Ms. Lawson?"

"I didn't want to go out, but Pookie needed a wee and she wouldn't go outside without me. I was able to get outside. I mean we've got small drifts blocking the door. She ran off into the snow. I had to chase her down. Found her, shivering, her back paws were bloody. I thought she had cut herself, you know on the ice. She's not a young pup any more and I have to—"

"Yes, Ms. Lawson, but what about the monolith?"

"That's where Pookie ran up to. She was standing, digging in a snow drift right behind the monolith, which is across from my house. Pookie was about halfway into the drift, lucky she's a samoyed. They love the snow. Anyway, how she did it, I don't know, but there was a man's arm or something sticking out of the snow. I thought he froze himself to death – but there was so much blood."

"Thank you Ms. Lawson. The police are on the scene behind me. There had been reports of shots fired last night and a police officer, name not yet released, was dispatched to the scene. We do not yet know if the remains uncovered by Pookie are of the officer who went missing after the call; he never reported from the scene. Or, if the remains are unconnected. As for right now, I've got to get back inside before I freeze as the New Jersey's Snowmageddon has claimed at least one life. That's Toni Yates reporting from the Jersey Shore."

ACT II
2012

BULLETIN
TROPICAL STORM SANDY ADVISORY NUMBER......2
NWS NATIONAL HURRICANE CENTER MIAMI FL....AL182012
500 PM EDT MON OCT 22 2012

...DEPRESSION STRENGTHENS INTO TROPICAL STORM
SANDY...

DISCUSSION AND 48-HOUR OUTLOOK

AT 500 PM EDT...2100 UTC...THE CENTER OF TROPICAL
STORM SANDY WAS LOCATED NEAR LATITUDE 12.5
NORTH...LONGITUDE 78.5 WEST. SANDY IS NEARLY
STATIONARY...BUT A MOTION TOWARD THE NORTH AND
NORTH-NORTHEAST IS EXPECTED DURING THE NEXT COUPLE
OF DAYS. ON THE FORECAST TRACK...THE CENTER WILL BE
NEAR OR OVER JAMAICA ON WEDNESDAY.

REPORTS FROM AN AIR FORCE HURRICANE HUNTER PLANE
INDICATE THAT THE MAXIMUM SUSTAINED WINDS HAVE
INCREASED TO NEAR 40 MPH...65KM/H...WITH HIGHER
GUSTS. ADDITIONAL STRENGTHENING IS FORECAST DURING
THE NEXT 48 HOURS...AND SANDY COULD BE NEAR
HURRICANE STRENGTH WHEN IT APPROACHES JAMAICA.

INTERESTS IN EASTERN CUBA AND THE BAHAMAS SHOULD
MONITOR THE PROGRESS OF SANDY.

FOR STORM INFORMATION SPECIFIC TO YOUR AREA...PLEASE
MONITOR PRODUCTS ISSUED BY YOUR NATIONAL
METEOROLOGICAL SERVICE.

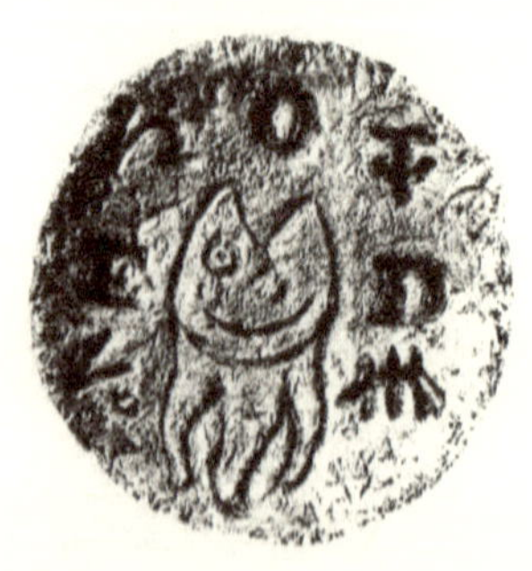

JEREMIAH

I had the dream again. Waves tearing into the shore. The storm seething, a convulsing maelstrom eating away at the coast. This time though, my hair fell in long dreadlocks; they wrapped around my neck in the winds like brown snakes. I know it was a serious dream, but I felt like laughing. I could see myself and everything around me at the same time and I looked like some male millennial Medusa, standing there arms outstretched, naked to the waist. I wore what I can only describe as a half robe or a sarong. It was the color of the storm around me, white and black and grey, patterned over with some serpentine ornamentation. Where the embroidery ended, my tattoos began. Twisting, twining, circling me. I was more muscular than I am now, maybe a good twenty or thirty pounds of muscle, which made me doubt for a moment who I was looking at.

But it was me. My skin took on the same shades as the cloth and the clouds. My face seemed painted though with some white ochre, which trailed down, weaving across my neck, chest and arms. My beard wasn't the scruff I have now; it was braided, in a long goatee like some Viking warrior. It curled almost to my chest, which was laced with what I initially thought was a vine pattern. On closer inspection, I saw they were the tentacles of a vast squid spreading upward.

I don't have tattoos or dreads. Not yet.

The dream-me stood at the monolith, a wisp of parchment in his hands. The parchment had one of those fish with the tentacles in brilliant blue ink, which almost exactly matched a tattoo on his back. Both were the only bit of color and seemed to glow with an eldritch light. Looking at him, I knew he was me, but he was him: the me-yet-to-be. On his back, the fish-head pointed up with the tentacles extending down, the letters EOD and curious runes closing around it. The black squid on his chest was in opposition, but with a similar runic device encircling the creature.

If this is a prescience, then I might have to start growing my hair and find a tattoo artist. Maybe start working out....

Musing over the dream, I ran my fingers across my nearly bald scalp, taking note of how undernourished my arms and hands looked. Right now, I couldn't be bothered by mundane things like muscles, hair, or even a shower while out here on my quest, my journey, my geas. So, before clearing out of the flat on Sentinel Street, I shaved it all. Now, I feel a bit like Jean Luc Picard, except more angular. I threw away my razors and won't buy any more before loading up the car and driving back to Jersey. That was my last shower too, but that's all prosaic stuff.

I grabbed a stick lying near my foot; it was jutting out from the remains of the campfire I had built late yesterday afternoon. I traced the designs and runes in the cooling ash, trying not to be annoyed with myself for leaving all my emergency supplies back in the car. I did have my jacket, a bottle of water, and my knife, but it wasn't until I was in the woods, here by the lake as the sun was already drifting down behind me, that I realized I would need more than my drab field jacket to keep warm. I was able to make a nice fire here on the strip of beach, shielded by a small stand of pines with the forest shielding me from the rest of humanity. It was quiet. What I needed. Despite the autumn chill. I remembered some of my survival skills. Before night set in, I made a bed of pine boughs, warmed the sand beneath with some hot rocks from the fire, built a nice trench alongside my bed, which I filled with some hot coals. I had been warm enough for most of the night. I suppose, as dickish as Marvin was, he did a decent thing by signing up for Tom Brown's Tracker Family Camp. That was a nice memory... in spite of Marvin. MJ came with. It was maybe two years before her father had died? He had been with us too. Donna was too prim to attend. I did learn more than a few things that have stuck with me all these years. Being able to build a fire yesterday and keep it most of the night? I shouldn't scoff at that. It helped.

I don't know what I was thinking when I parked the car and trekked down here. I just wanted to see the water. Here.

Grasping the stick, I kept tracing the designs from my dream, wishing I hadn't left my notebooks back at the car along with my emergency kit. I guess I was more upset by everything... way more than I thought....though I wasn't about to go home. Not now. Not yet. I needed a place to think. Maybe tonight I'll find a room somewhere.

MJ's still at school. I'm not going back there anytime soon. Who remembers where her mother was living now? Not in Toms River. So there's no reason for MJ to come down here. The last people I want to see right now are Donna and Marvin. So, why the fuck come back to NJ anyway?

Doodle. Scratch. E. O. D.

Seems right somehow. I'm surprised I hadn't thought of them before now....I mean, other than a few units at school.... I mean, in Professor McKittrick's Global Religions class, he insisted they were defunct, but we learned about them anyway, like we would the Picts or Cathars. I wonder though. I suppose what I've been seeing is a version of their sigil. I never thought about becoming one of them, much less swimming off to Y'ha-nthlei. I really don't know why I didn't think of them before. It's unsettling how my mind works— or doesn't work. Maybe MJ's right. Maybe I am going off my nut.

My swimming isn't great either. So there's that.

Tattoos never occurred to me though. But, I suppose, for power, for purpose. Maybe. But, I don't know about one of those fish things. I'm not opposed, but... The squid seemed somehow wrong. Anyway... I wouldn't presume E.O.D. Not solo. Not unless they find me... or I find them?

The runes at any rate were more than interesting. I tried tracing them from memory, but what I drew in the cinders and sand also seemed wrong. Unholy. Not as intended.

Those fish-heads though.... I suppose they have been a sort of totem for me, but not with the E.O.D. emblazoned around them. I keep seeing them. Just them. The tentacled fish-heads. In reality. Not just in my dreams and waking visions. They started on my genealogical material from Orne back when I was in intermediate school.... I didn't see them for years and years after that. Lately though, they've been more frequent, especially during my time at Miskatonic. With and without the runes. They were littered throughout the Marquis' writings when I first started studying at Orne. What was it, little more than a year ago? I was in my first semester there this time last year.

It's cliché, but that was a lifetime ago. Sometimes, I would see one in a watermark on the page when I'd hold it up to the light. Another time, it was right there, scribbled in pen under the return address from Miskatonic's Registrar. Again, I saw one on a professor's nameplate beside her office. While others had been carefully etched on a few tombstones in the cemetery at the old Burying Ground on Lich Street. One had been hastily scratched into one of the Starshmucks tables at 454 Sentinal Street; it stared up at me from beneath my macchiato with it's insensate eyes.

I wouldn't see the fish-heads every day, but I started to see them often enough. And, every time I would ask someone, pointing attention to the sign, they would laugh it off and divert me to some other topic or look at me in disbelief. Like I was the crazy one. Like in the library, when I saw them scattered about carved into the shelves themselves and I demanded Ms. Green explain why there were so many of these fish-heads and what did they mean? She simply sat there, staring at me. She did whistle for Napoleon, the watchdog who I secretly believed was nothing short of a hellhound. She sat there placidly, stroking the dog's gargantuan head, while I tried pointing them out to her.

Another time, right before that premiere incident in the library with Dr. Danforth, MJ's advisor, and the psilocybin truffles, I found more than a few fish-heads clustered together, inscribed on texts in the library stacks. I didn't say a word to the implacable Ms. Green. I tried taking photos of them with my phone, but gave up. The photos never focused well or when I did succeed in capturing one digitally, whenever I tried later to retrieve the image to show MJ or a Professor, or anyone really, the image would disappear off my phone. So, I gave up trying to document them, other than mentally.

Over my three terms at Miskatonic, these symbols led me to investigate all sorts of stuff that went so far beyond MJ's D&D campaigns. I became Curwen. For real. Taking back my name along with the magickal practice that is my birthright.... There at school, I found the symbol helped me to refine which texts I should focus my attentions on. Sometimes, I would wander the stacks, tracing my fingers along the spines, lighting on a specific volume when I saw the symbol. Other times, I would see the tentacled fish-heads sprinkled throughout town, sometimes in shop windows. Once inside, I would always come to a discernment, usually amidst a torrent of knowledge. The shops were always bookstores, apothecaries, botanica, antique shops with a penchant for the occult. Once the shop turned out to be a headshop, which was the only time the symbol didn't immediately lead me true. When I am able to afford it, cannabis is a primary medicine for me, so in that sense the symbol didn't lie. But, there was nothing in that shop except hookahs and bongs. I did wonder if there wasn't something in the back room that the shop clerk didn't want to tell me about... That was the whole reason I swiped Dr. Danforth's truffles. I saw the image above the box. So, I secreted them away while I waited for MJ to finish her shift as the doctor's intern. Those chocolates became a nice part of my medicine. I never fessed up to MJ though, but she knew...

Most of the time, despite my inability to photograph the fish-heads, the image was there, in reality. On a display, a window decal, sometimes etched onto the door, on the sidewalk in front, or beside the shop window in chalk. Like those symbols hobos would draw for other knights of the road by way of warning or invitation. Once or twice, just before I left Arkham, I began to see them in my mind, a phantasmal phosphorescence suspended in the air. Now and again, the symbol would still be there after I left the shop.

It never occurred to me that I imagined any of them. Not until the library... but... I erased what I had been scratching into the ash and sand with my foot and started anew. I tried getting the symbols right as I thought, turning over the dream and my path up until now in my mind. I needed to see the patterns if I was going to puzzle this all together.

Overall, following the signs, they became more helpful in developing a serious practice than the earlier dabbling I had done with the Tarot and rune casting, before Arkham. They also led me outside of the typical stuff we studied in school: the Kabbalah, The Bahir, Sefer Yetzirah, The Golden Dawn, and John Dee. All which I studied incessantly. I found between my school studies and following the symbol, I traced a long swath in esoterica, absorbing everything I could possibly get my hands on: shamanism, witchcraft, Wicca, Asatru, other paths, from Crowley to Culpepper, Flamel to Mathers, Cunningham to Kondratiev, Grof to McKenna. Of course, several of my professors had us focus on the *Al Azif* and Thelemic Orders. At the time, I didn't harmonize with the "bugges by night" way of looking at the world. I found myself resonating more with indigenous medicine practices, which could be one of the reasons Miskatonic gave me my walking papers, aside from the psilocin-laced chocolates Dr. Danforth accused me of stealing. Which I did, but that's not the point. No one acknowledged that they were meant to be mine. The sigil told me to take them.

No matter how much the fuddies at Miskatonic fashion themselves as being a bastion of diversity and intellectual freedom, they don't take kindly to certain aspects of herb and plant lore. Especially when used for mental and physical well being. Particularly when that medicine is illegal in most of the lower 48. Though, Danforth didn't have a problem with microdosing like they do in Silicon Valley. I suppose, when used as a performance enhancer, that's fine. When used to throw open the doors to the mind's mystical dimensions, when being *used* instead of just studied like some case notes or a blip in a textbook, Miskatonic is as obstinate as anywhere else.

I can say, one of my prepubescent goals was achieved, however, when I declared for a degree in Occult Studies, with my concentration in Ancient and Medieval Magics. Over the last few years, even before Miskatonic, I took a hard leaning toward working with Shamans, Curanderos, Ayahuasqueros, and Priestesses. That was on my own, though. I was either cast aside as being too young, or when I was older I had no one to initiate me. Not really. There was that moment with the whiskey jug on the shores of Crystal Lake all those years ago.... but those were Marvin's people. The Allens. They weren't my people. Not my family. Not my friends.

While at school, both before and during Miskatonic, I didn't have many of those, beyond MJ. She was my lifeline. Finding groups who met after hours at a yoga studio, in the basement of a community center, or in the back rooms of occult shops wasn't that hard. During my time in Arkham, I followed the traces of them on my mind. But, there wasn't anyone to really learn from. I modeled here and there. I observed. Mostly, I have been left to myself to learn the ways of fine tuning my mind and body with natural planetary rhythms and cosmic energies... which didn't quite fit with my school learning. Though they did have some wonderful units on Occult Theory and Practical Application. I felt Professor Greene's class glossed over too much, though. It was only one class when it should have been a concentration, a series of workshops. Learning from a tome is grand, in a wizarding school sort of way. But, I had to pursue my own path, augmenting my academic studies with tactile experiences which really can't be duplicated in the classroom. Their "practical application" didn't have us doing more than wave our arms around and mumble chants. They knew nothing about zeroing in the senses to truly observe the realm of spirit. I have to admit, I did learn more from books and online communities than from any specific group or person. I carved out my own practice, which led me here and led me to him. I'm sure he will be my teacher and already I can feel my awareness, my mental skills, my observational talents have sharpened as a result of my own studies and since meeting both of them in my dreams.

Combined with the ancient Yogic breath techniques I picked up and the mudras, which help enormously, I believe I can now eliminate mental and physical stresses caused by any number of negative stimuli. I found while I was at school, I became easily distracted. Especially in a town like Arkham where the dead energies cluster, seeping into the very fabric of the architecture, making it all coruscate with an unholy light. But, lately, maybe because of my application of those truffles, I have been able to focus, narrow my breath, extricate maleficia, clear away the dead energy.

I used the last truffle last night. That sucks.

While I was at school, as I focused on and strengthened my senses, I came to recognize a variation in the energies as I travelled the city. Hell even traveling across the college's sprawling campus. The energies were clusters of people who practice the magickal arts. I could see them, like a ghostly smudge across my vision, where they congregated, their covens, their temples. I knew when magickal practice was taking place, and I could separate that from more mundane paranormal activity, which appeared to me as a glow rather than a smudge, an overlay to my site.

I keenly recall the first time I walked across campus, early in the Fall semester, before the tentacled fish began leading me to shamans' alchemies and ancient practices. I rounded the corner between University and Manning Hall and saw a pile of amputated limbs, some still quivering and steaming in a crisp winter morning. There was snow beneath and surrounding them, an ungodly red spreading, the air took on a metallic tang, and I heard dim screams from the upper windows of the building. I shook my head, scoured my eyes with my palms, and looked again. There they were, still heaped alongside the red brick, beneath the plaque dedicated to the memory of poor Dr. Halsey. I remember walking forward, in a daze, reaching out my hands to the mass which glowed ever so slightly, thinking I would be able to touch them. Only I scuffed my hands on the bricks, which were warm in the late summer sun. I blinked, seeing my scraped hands and the unblemished ground beneath my feet, grass brown from the heat, but I also saw, in a distorted overlay, the limbs and blood on the snow. During freshmen orientation, later that day, I learned that University Hall had been a hospital during the Revolution.

Yet, as I pursued my degree, I found my blood calling, my family, my ancestors, and these fish-totems all pulled me to the other side of the magickal spectrum. I think the whole mess with Miskatonic has put me on this trajectory. I have to laugh, again. While at school, I wanted to and did pursue a more wholesome, healing foundation to my practice. MJ always said studying at Miskatonic, pursuing a career there after our classwork, would be tantamount to becoming an Auror. We studied the Dark Arts in order to deter, desist, or detain. But, as everything piled on, as the messages from home—chastising, humiliating, infantalizing me combined with the endless cautions and probations and disciplines from the university? I turned to face that terror by night, that nocturnal sound, the insectile, demonic howl I often saw smudged across my vision. I needed to turn back toward the ancestral pull of my background of evil verisimilitude.

Now, I think he will help me. Now, I have found my teacher.

I find myself tired. So very tired of the ignorant fools that prance and preen and call themselves kin. They are not blood. Not my blood. Donna, Marvin, and their congregation of simpering friends. They've been an albatross since I was a kid. Always there. Always in the background. Whenever I had a moment of crisis, either of the two Allens or one of their close group of compatriots would be there, trying to influence some decision or some outcome, which should have been of my own devising.

Now, I think the dream is the final key. I've got to move outward, toward the coast, see if I can find another signpost to lead me to logical next steps, or any conclusion. Maybe there is a place for me in the Order...

I've had the dream in many variations, but none as detailed, clear or precise as the one I had here, last night, on the shores of Crystal Lake, on the three-way crossroads of the aptly named Bone Hill Road. It only confirms my place on this path. I heard the words whispered from the mind of the me-him. He wants me to find him. To pursue the path as full Brujo. No more of this love and light, inner peace and understanding. It's all bullshit.

But, then He came. The Father. My All-Father. His voice joined with mine and the urge is even stronger than it was before.

I stood there in the dream, the me-yet-to-be, a glory of my being. My skin mottled from tattoos and ochre. My screams devoured by the storm pummeling me. The parchment tore from my grasp. The sea yawned, revealing His face. A towering mass of silver, gold, and emerald. He rose, gargantuan, before me, like the Kraken from *Clash of the Titans.* I wanted to laugh, to cry, but I was frozen by His gaze and the bubbling, churning sea as He continued to rise.

I knew I was no longer there in the dream. I couldn't have been. I would have been swallowed entirely by the hulking wave. His eyes were two convex discs, golden, the size of my car. An undulating frill of emerald and black capped His head. His mouth set with row upon row of silver teeth twice my height. All sound was dead in my ears. I couldn't hear Him, but felt a pressure in my mind as he beckoned me to find Him. As He emanated from the depths of the ocean, I saw pythonic spires rise beside and behind Him. Peaked, twisting, spiked towers of red and black stone with doorways, arches, staircases of impossible angles, with creatures standing here and there, watching me, watching him. They were uncannily like the MJ's blasted Sahuagin and very much like smaller versions of Him: bulbous, frog eyes, webbed hands, more frog-like than fish. Some were robed in glorious sweeping textiles like feathered seaweed, but crusted with jewels and shot with gold. I suspect they are His priests and priestesses. They all had reptilian frills or spine sails like some fish-frog dimetrodon.

One stood just to the left and a little behind the All-Father. He seemed to shine with his own infernal light. He wore a crown on his misshapen head. It looked like some dull, golden coral, twisted into horns. He wore a crude necklace of what looked like rope, upon which hung a disc of stone bearing the identical symbol to the tattoo and the parchment the dream-me bore. I knew him to be my ancestor. The Marquis D'Bourget.

A thrumming radiated throughout the dream, from the air, the sea, the storm and from Father Dagon. It was wordless but engulfed me, in a shroud, protecting me from the storm, both the dream me and the dreaming me. The All-Father opened His maw and a small shard of stone glittered against the void of His mouth. I couldn't tell what color it rightly was. It seemed like bleached bone, but it could have been stone or a tarnished metal. It was a tablet of some kind. In the dream I could zero in my vision, like an eagle, zooming in to focus. The tablet wasn't rectangular, but an odd shape, like a medieval herald or shield, sides curving in places, angled in others. There was a repeated pattern bisecting the thing and surrounding it's outer edges. I realized the pattern was a language. One I couldn't hope to understand. Not now. Not yet. I couldn't properly make out the images on either side of the center text, not because I couldn't see them. I don't yet recognize what I was looking at. One looked like a barrel with a starfish on top and tentacles or seaweed circling it; the other looked like a conglomeration of eyes, punctuated here and there by a preponderance of teeth.

I woke with a voice in my mind which said simply: *Brujo, find us by the signs.*

I suppose I've come this far, I should follow through to the judgement. Whatever that may be.

When I woke, I needed to integrate, to sit still, to breathe. But my mind wasn't still. A surge of rage exploded as my first thought wasn't the intensity of the dream.

I wished I had my old tent.

I was cold and damp and the fire had gone out. I wanted my old tent with such a ferociousness, I was momentarily averted because of that damned tent. The one dickhead Marvin had tossed out with the trash so long ago. He had said the zippers were broken the morning after our last camping trip to Crystal Lake, seven years ago, the fall right before that insane blizzard in '05. I overheard him when we came home; he was telling Donna that he wondered if it wasn't glowing.

Why think of that now?

I continued to doodle in the ash and figured: instead of push away my waking thoughts, I needed to embrace them, acknowledge them, and in so doing, integrate them and perhaps push past them. They had to come to me for a reason.

Ok. So, the fucking tent. I suppose it would be natural for that to pop up. This is where we used to come. That stretch of sand there, behind me. Right in front of the treeline and sometimes we'd set up our camp right inside the forest, depending on how many of us there were. Here, at Crystal Lake. Marvin used to laugh and call it Manchester Township's own blue lagoon. Most of the time we'd come down here, we actually did camp. It was nice, especially the times MJ came with. There were a few truly memorable times.

But that particular trip, the one I woke thinking about, I seemed to irritate one of Marvin's friends. This weird old guy who called himself "Uncle Zadok," even though Marvin told him not to. I didn't know why at the time. I wouldn't know why the name Zadok Allen would have upset Marvin, not until later, after I went to Miskatonic. "Uncle Zadok" had been visiting from New England and wasn't one of Marvin's regular camping buddies.

Usually, when we'd all camp, there would be some actual camping involved. Grilling. Swimming, even though I really couldn't at the time. MJ would try to teach me. We'd all go foraging in the woods, especially if it was morel season. It was like the renegade Boy Scouts because we weren't allowed to camp there. It was private property, abandoned, but still, not a public camping site. But there weren't regular patrols or anything of the kind. Sometimes we'd fish, too. Back in the 90's some locals introduced fish to the lake. Trout I think. No one asked if we should be eating the fish from Crystal Lake, because it wasn't a proper lake, but a remnant from the old mineral mines which dot the pine barrens. Swimming was risky there too, but the adults did and I tried. It had been years since anyone went missing in the lake, but every so often, kids did drown. The shore would end abruptly, maybe a dozen yards into the water, into a sheer drop. It went from wading to over 30 feet down on that first shelf. The middle of the lake seemed bottomless and no one went out that far. Not swimming. The water was too damned cold.

During that trip, which was the shortest and the last, "Uncle Zadok" spent his time getting mildly shitfaced with Marvin, while I tried teaching myself to swim in the Bahama-blue lake. There were maybe two more of Marvin's friends there, but no one got in the water and I seemed to be an afterthought, until the sun went down. MJ wasn't with us and there weren't any other kids. It was just me in the fucking woods with maybe four grown men. I spent most of my time wading, wandering, or just sitting in my tent. Lucky it was only an overnight. They had built a fire as the afternoon lengthened, but they just sat there... after they got the fire going, continuing to drink... but this time, it wasn't Coors or any elephant piss from a can. After sunset, they sat drinking something harder. All the while, they stared at me, muttering to themselves so I couldn't hear, watching the sun set. As it went down, I changed into dry clothes in my tent, partly to escape their stare, and then when my stomach wouldn't stop growling, I went to sit with them by the fire, thinking dinner would be at hand. They were on their way to getting roaring drunk and had started some kind of weird pep rally or something right as the night took hold.

That was all before I started my genealogical probings, before I had any magickal understanding whatsoever. Funny, I haven't thought about that night in forever and a day. Had I, I might have recognized that they were doing something with an intent. The men had been drinking some foul smelling liquor from an old fashioned whiskey jug they kept passing around. It smelled like rotten fish. I refused to try it when Marvin and one of the others, whose name and face have long been forgotten, offered me some. When I asked about dinner, they only laughed and handed me the jug, which I tossed back at them.

"Uncle Zadok" didn't ask. He simply held me down and forced a few mouthfuls on me, as Marvin and the others laughed. I spat it out, and he repeated until I swallowed enough to make him happy. The stuff made me gag. It tasted like the inside of an old barrel that had been used to house sardines that had gone off. I wanted to vomit, but "Uncle Zadok" told me I couldn't for at least a half hour. He told me to hold it in my belly until it was time. He said I would know when I couldn't hold it any longer.

I tried plunging my fingers down my throat, but they stopped me. The nameless men. Marvin let them hold my arms and keep me seated by the firelight for more than three-quarters of an hour, well past the time the old bastard (who insisted I also call him "Uncle Zadok", even when I told him I didn't have a fucking uncle) had told me to hold onto whatever that sludge had been. I got him back though, when a torrent of black ichor came up in his face almost an hour after he had forced it on me. After that, they continued what I can now call their ritual and let me go. I sat on the sand a little away from them and noticed how black the sky had become. No moon. No star. No cloud either. Just black as though a pall had been cast over the heavens. With the vast lake and the forest circling us, we were the only people left in the world. The forest was silent. I had been swallowed by a black hole. No sounds except the men's asinine chanting, their whoops, and attempts at what I can only now call throat-singing, punctured the night. I left them to their business and went to my tent, feeling queasy, fevered, and as though I was the loneliest person ever.

That was the moment my attitude towards the Allens really changed. Before that I had called them Mom and Dad. I never made that mistake again.

The next morning Marvin kept complaining about the sheer yellowness of the tent. One of nameless accomplices told him, as they were packing up camp, that Sarco, the company that had owned and mined the area, had closed down because of radioactive contamination. Up until that point, Marvin hadn't seemed to care that over the years, kids who had tried swimming in crystal waters had turned up dead, or never had turned up at all because they had sunk like stones in the too-blue, too-cold water. And radioactive contamination? Wouldn't he have known if the company that had operated this site had mined for some radioactive substance? Wouldn't there have been radiation warnings? I have been down here easily half a dozen times in my life and not once have I ever seen any posted warnings except two. No trespassing. No hunting. That was it.

I often wondered if Marvin wanted me there with him on that moonless camping trip just to see if I would drown too. Maybe that had been the intention of the trip? Maybe I was supposed to drown? Was I some bizarre sacrifice?

I never saw "Uncle Zadok" again, but whenever I asked Marvin about him, he shouted at me to get in my room and keep out of his business. Donna didn't want to hear me either when I told her about the old fart forcing me to drink alcohol or that the others, who I also never saw again either, had held me down. But, the idea of a radioactive tent? No. Marvin was fine with everything else, but when we were getting gas at Wawa on 37, he just tossed my tent into a dumpster.

Either way, I did like those trips. Before that last one. Despite Marvin's being an infernal asshole, despite being forced to drink whatever the fuck. I loved the quiet of this place. Maybe that's why I came here yesterday.

I sat, cross-legged, left hand curling in the Heart Mudra, my right hand comfortable in Jnana Mudra and I breathed away the anger, the resentment, the disgust, the roiling turmoil in my gut. In. One, two, three. Hold. One, two, three. Out. One, two, three.

Lidding my eyes, I watched the sun climb over the rim of the trees as the early morning shadows lengthened across the white sand around my impromptu campsite.

I came here wanting some semblance of my past. Something, no matter how fractured, to see if I can make sense of my now and see into my future. No. I shouldn't have slept rough on the ground. It got pretty cold last night and I don't know what the fuck I was thinking. I kept breathing, allowing the anger to rise, but releasing it in short bursts. Slowly as the sun rose, my mind seemed to still. I thought no more about Marvin or "Uncle Zadok", their fucking jug or my yellow fucking tent.

In. One, two, three. Hold. One, two, three. Out. One, two, three.

They told me Brujo.... which means one thing to me. Chaos. An unfurling of the cosmos to come crashing down on their heads. I can hear the relentless prattle in my mind: Marvin laughing, Donna cajoling, their leering. Why else remember *"Uncle Zadok"* and what Marvin let him do if not to put paid to any debts, any encumbrances? They owe me. I am a Curwen after all. I have the blood of mystery in my veins and the Allens will regret that last night by Crystal Lake.

In. One, two, three. Hold. One, two three. Out. One, two three.

Last night's dream revealed the Marquis. A rendering of him...but still. It was him. Could he have been one of those fish-frogs? How? He had been human once. So, EOD. It must be. The sudden realization snapped almost audibly in my being. It was like a metallic, cosmic whoosh. Sort of like those truffles, when I took three of them at once the weekend MJ went off with her quasi-beau Jaimie.

Without warning, as with the damned tent, an anguish surfaced in my mind. I regretted getting myself booted from school. I needed to know more. I couldn't hope to learn about the Order alone. I should have kept my mouth shut, read the assignments, did the work. Kept my other path to myself. Not got in Dr. Danforth's face.

But how could I have ignored the signs?

In. One, two, three. Hold. One, two three. Out. One, two three.

In. One, two, three. Hold. One, two three. Out. One, two three.

I have to integrate the two. I have to follow the signs and bring myself back to my origins. The Marquis and the Curwen line. They both, for lack of a better term, were Brujo. I suppose as blood calls to blood that should be my path. Maybe I should start where the Marquis left off? Where he was last seen? Pelican Island. Down Route 37. I read in my genealogical odyssey that the Marquis was held prisoner, after the whole Long Island Beach Massacre. That was a given. But, why did he get involved with the whole highway robbery thing? The Marquis had been after occult documents... Perhaps I share more with him? After really delving the material at Orne, after doing my own research and coming to my conclusion that the darker path isn't necessarily the wrong path, I believe the Marquis may have been driven as I have been, by the signs and that symbol. He was on a quest. Not so very different than my own, perhaps. I should follow his path. Why else come back to New Jersey? I could have stayed back in Arkham. MJ wouldn't have minded.

In. One, two, three. Hold. One, two three. Out. One, two three.

The Marquis had been held prisoner on Pelican Island. I believe he escaped, that he wasn't executed alongside the others. There was no record of him except there had been a letter between him and Crane, but that had been dated after the Marquis had been arrested. So, he had to have escaped... but to what end? He couldn't have just vanished.

I need to get to the coast, to Pelican Island. But I also know the clouds and the rage in the wind, the rising sea from the dreams... All that isn't just Father Dagon calling to me. That part of the dream I have been seeing for weeks. Last night was the first time I truly saw myself and truly saw the All-Father. In the other dreams, I would see the priests or priestesses. I might hear their chants and see some*thing* rise. Sometimes it was a city, like an Atlantis, but imagined by a decrepit and unsound mind, unholy angles, etched with writing that would cause the mind to unravel were the veracity of the words to ever be uttered or known. In each dream, the storm was evident. After last night's dream, not only do I know my path, I also know the storm is coming. Now. It will be here soon and I must go find the spot in my dream before it arrives.

I resolved to go back and get the car. I can get the rest of my stuff. At least, what I need at any rate. There shouldn't be a problem leaving the car somewhere, start the pilgrimage the way it's supposed to be: on foot. Getting the inkling to park behind the high school over on Colonial Drive wasn't too bad. But, I should've gone and gotten a few things last night. Then again, what comfort does an ascetic need?

My stomach rumbled. My nose was cold and my crotch itched from what I hoped was sand in my pants and not poison ivy or sand-fleas. It had been a few days since I showered.... and roughing it in the car hasn't been so great...Ascetic indeed. I was more than lucky I had a lighter in my jacket and actually knew how to build a fire last night.

My stomach ached. As much as I wanted to pursue an ascetic path, giving up meals, shelter, and basic amenities, I needed a shower. I thought about options and opted on breakfast before anything else.

UNION CAFE: LAKEHURST, NJ

"He's back, Sofie. The bald guy. Whole fucking place smells like armpits now," Angie puffed an errand strand of hair, vicious red punctuating a crown of sable, out of her eyes.

"It's fine, Ange. The day is young. We love our *clientèle*. And smelly ones need java too. As long as he's calm this time. We're good. Dennis might stop in later if that makes you more comfortable."

"Seriously? I love you Sof, but they don't call me Horror Quinn because I need a dude to handle my battles. You either, Whipped Scream. This one here's freshmeat. We have a bout next week and it'll be good to get the grind on him, maybe practice a few blocks on the skinny little bastard. He looks like he hasn't been fed in a month. Maybe the last thing he ate was your Greens, Egg, and Ham waffle from yesterday morning. But, like you said, as long as he's calm. He should pay for that book though...” The taller woman hesitated before replacing the milk in the fridge to give her roller derby sister a half, shoulder hug, over the hissing steam wand, while whispering over the foaming milk: “What's he doing, now?”

“Sitting by your mural, again....” Sofie muttered, pausing as she finished making the latte to eyeball the lanky twentysomething. “—fuck *is* he doing?”

Today, he didn't come over to order. He had just swept into the café to plunk on the couch up front like he was in his own damned living-room. Twisting his head in a weird angle, he couldn't stop staring at Angie's mural. His eyes were fever-bright, like one of those public service announcements against drugs she used to see when she was a kid: eggs cracking into a pan. Sofie could imagine this is what your brain looked like on drugs. He even had the shakes as he suddenly jumped up from the couch to get closer to the wall painting. Fucking dude was weird. He tore an unused chair away from the table up front, not caring that an older Asian couple had been sitting there, quietly reading while sipping their matcha lattes. Usually, Sofie wasn't a person to note that someone else was “weird.” Who the fuck isn't? Shit, she was one who defined the term. Besides. This was New Jersey: the state of weird.

But this dude? Weird didn't cut it. He suddenly appeared maybe last week? And there he was, like any regular customer. Friendly. Smiling. Ordered. Stuck around most of the day with a pile of papers, notebooks, and a tablet he used for surfing, researching something, squinting at street views on Google Earth. She took note of how much this guy wrote, longhand, using an old fountain pen. She even chuckled, asking if he was a novelist. He smiled, but didn't respond. He left maybe a half hour later, right before closing, and she figured he wouldn't be coming back.

But, there he was again the next day. He looked as though he had been sleeping in his car. He bought lunch and left. Rinse. Repeat, every day for the next several days. He was practically living off their waffles, sammies, and lattes. Then, yesterday, he came in like his usual, which was anytime between 7am, when the café opened and noon, but minus his mobile office. Her other half, Dennis had just come in and instead of putting on music, Dennis opted for a repeat viewing of *The Office*, which was their usual thing. Sofie thought Dennis was being funny and maybe it was meant to be a little dig since The Union had become this wackadoodle's office. Often, the café crew would binge whatever their latest series was on their huge overhead projector. *The Office* was a fave. The guy came in yesterday like his usual, placed an order and went to the loo. When he came out, there was Michael Scott shrieking about something, his head about eight feet high on the projector. Everyone was laughing, customers, too. But bald weirdo started to have a kitten about what a stupid show. Sofie gave him his breakfast and he did calm down. But, maybe an hour later, he started getting more than a bit loud, muttering something about fish-frogs or something bizarre when he started thumbing through one of the café's many bookshelves, coming up with one of those old, pick-your-adventure books with a weird fish-person on the cover. Title started with an S and sounded like a disease. He had started carrying on about how it wasn't a proper novel, but a companion for a role-playing game. D&D maybe? Dennis had had enough and told the guy to piss off. Dude had the balls to take the fucking book too. Angie wanted to go after him, but Sofie thought if he wanted it that bad, let him have it. Maybe they would get lucky and not see him again.

Why didn't the guy just stay on the couch or sit at the bar table that was right there?

Here he was again, smelling like he hadn't showered in weeks. He didn't smell this bad yesterday. Maybe he slept with a skunk? Sofie coughed, mock-politeness, as the guy plopped his chair right up against Angie's mural— a sprawling mass of color adorning the wall immediately inside the café. It was the place's grand centerpiece: the head of a woman, about nine feet high. Sofie always thought of it as Dúfa of the Nine Sisters. Ægir's daughter. Goddess of the mists, there with her diadem of seashells and a shipwreck in her hair. This dude's nose was almost touching her hand, inspecting one of the painting's lower tentacles.

Coming around the counter, Sofie dragged another chair to replace the one he had taken.

Another ersatz cough. "Ordering anything today?" She asked him, but his attention was fixed on the painting. "Hello?" No reply. "Dude, we're an open place, but you can't bother the other customers and please don't press your nose against the mural. You also owe me for that book you took yesterday."

Come on guy, take a hint.

"When were these done?" Mostly, he ignored her. Still, inspecting, there with his face almost touching the wall. "These here." His momentary stillness shattered by him impulsively pointing at various points on the painting. He turned his frenzied eyes, flashing dark green, on her. She took a step back, almost falling over the older Asian woman who pretended the guy wasn't there. The woman's husband had been settling their bill at the counter with

Angie, who had been giving the guy the Horror Quinn look of death. Sofie always thought her fellow Jersey Shore Roller Girl looked more like Eric Draven than Harley Quinn when in full derby girl mode. Sofie never wanted to be on the receiving end of that look whether they were on or off the track.

"What now?" Sofie instinctively took a wide stance to block him, as though she was on the track instead of in her own café. Her fists balled up at her sides.

"These. Here." He got up slowly, perhaps sensing she was on the defense. *Clueless much?*

Cocking his head to the side, uncannily like her neighbor's Jack Russell terrier, he pointed first to the cup in portrait's hand, the cup bearing the café's logo. A small symbol had been scratched into the drop of coffee on the logo just beneath the "U" for Union Café. The symbol was almost hidden beside the titaness' thumb. It looked like a Jesus-fish, but with tentacles. Once Sofie registered what it was, the guy pointed to other areas in the mural: beside the conch-shaped ear, in one of the shells in the crown, the largest across the topsail of the ship in her hair.

When the fuck did this happen? Sofie was pissed.

"What'd you do, guy? Mess up all Angie's work? We've been cool but—"

He held up both hands. One of them curled in one of those hand gestures they teach you in yoga class.

Shaking his head, he murmured an apology: "I only noticed them. I didn't do this. I merely noticed. I apologize." He bowed slightly, placing his other hand, in another twirling hand gesture, across his heart.

Sofie snorted, wanted to turn away, but didn't want to turn her back to him.

"You going to order anything? Yesterday my partner had to ask you to leave and you stole a book from the shelf. I'm slapping $5 on your tab for the book, k?" Sofie said, backing toward the counter, which she ducked behind. "You going to be calmer? Can I get you your usual, the greens and waffle with what a latte?"

Nod. Yes.

"Fine. Have a seat. You're more than welcome to take the couch. You can observe Angie's masterpiece all you want, just don't lean on it. Especially not your nose." Sofie made a harumphing noise. "I'll have your order in a minute."

Nod. Fine.

"Ok. You got a name, guy? You've been here every day for a week. How about telling us who you are?"

"Jeremiah." His disused voice crackled as he scratched several large mosquito bites dotting his head.

Sofie could see his raw scalp and she got the crippities, as her mother would call the creeps. *God I hope he doesn't have fleas.* Suddenly she heard Scully singing "Jeremiah was a bullfrog" from one of her favorite episodes of *The X-files.* She supposed maybe they should start binging that next. But, they'd have to skip over the really gross episodes otherwise it might put off some of their clientèle.

"Do you know how the signs got on the mural?" Guy asked. *Jeremiah.* That's what his name was. Bullfrog boy. Sofie shrugged.

Banging down a mug a bit too heavily on the counter, Angie interjected, "Those didn't show up until you did. I didn't put anything like that in my work. I've never seen those before." She didn't try to hide how desperately she wanted to smack the guy across his bug-bitten noggin with the mug.

"Do you have security footage?" He pointed to a camera positioned over the door.

"It's just a dummy. We haven't gotten it hooked up yet," Sofie said, kicking herself mentally as Angie came up and pinched her arm. *Now the fucker's going to come rob us.*

He shook his head. "No. I'm not like that."

Did he hear her? *Fuck.*

Pointing to the mug and plate Angie had just placed on the counter, he asked if she minded wrapping them to go. "I'm not staying after all. And I suggest you leave as well."

"Fuck, dude. Seriously?" Angie blurted out, spatula in hand. She really was going to slap him now.

Shaking his head again. "You misunderstand me. There's a storm coming. It's bigger than anything that's been seen here in a long time. Move inland. Far inland. It'll be here in a week's time."

Right. Loony toons. One minute he's mister crazy pants, his nose pressed to the mural, twitching like he's got the Dts. Next, he's a goddamn Yoda, all zen and shit.

Sofie helped Angie finish dude's order. He handed them a twenty and two fives when his phone rang. Motioning for them to keep the change, he took his breakfast and his phonecall out the door.

"Don't let the door hit you," Angie grumbled despite the tip. "Big spender. Hmph. Storm my ass. Can we just tell him we're closed if he comes back tomorrow?"

JEREMIAH & MJ

"Hey MJ. You never guess what I found you a copy of: *The Slayer's Guide to Sahuagin.* It was in a little cafe out here—"

"Thanks but, what the fuck did you do to your hair, Jerry? You scruffy nerfherder. What's that a beard, *Jerry?*" She did her best Elaine voice from *Seinfeld.*

"Please don't call me that." Jeremiah exited the cafe and stood aside on the sidewalk. He didn't mind talking on the phone. But since he left school, MJ kept insisting on video chatting with him, so she could check up on him. She said it let her see if he was eating or sleeping. He hated facetiming or whatever it was she called it. He never knew how to handle the phone, look at it, and walk at the same time. So he just stood there, breakfast in one hand, other arm extended upward, craning his neck to look up.

"*Jerry* what the fuck? Relax your arm. Who taught you how to hold a fucking phone? And tell me where did you sleep last night? Not home I take it. Your car? The woods?"

"I have no home MJ."

"Don't be a drama queen, Jeremiah. Why are you back in

Jersey if you have no home? You could have just stayed at the flat. Then I could keep an eye on you. There was no reason in the world for you to leave. We have the room. It was yours. Now I have to find another roommate. Thanks dick."

"You know why I left. I couldn't. You didn't understand and neither did my advisors."

"But you weren't expelled. You were placed on a temporary leave for mental health reasons. You're still matriculated. They'll let you come back to school next term, after you display some initiative. Maybe finish the work Dr. Greene gave you. Do the work from Professor Neal and old Rice. They'll give you a chance."

"I've got a different goal right now. I have to follow the trail of breadcrumbs and find my teacher—"

"But, that's what I'm telling you, *Jeremiah.* Your teachers are back at school. They're giving you a chance. Do you honestly think you were the first student to go crackers? *Lux in Obscuro Sumus.* You don't think the darkness overwhelms the light at times?"

"Fine. Yes. You're absolutely right—"

"Stop being an asshole, Jeremiah." MJ narrowed her eyes at him the way she used to glare at him over the top of the campaign maps she would use as a partition dividing the dungeon master from the rest of the party. She was always DM. He never had the patience for it. She always glared at him like that, especially when he was fucking up one of her campaigns. "What are you doing right now?"

"I just got breakfast." He held up his coffee cup, a brown bag awkwardly held in the same hand. "Can't I call you like a normal person? I hate chatting like this. Or text me. That's fine."

"Then you'll just blow up my phone with stupid dancing babies and Mr. Bean. Make me think everything is fine. Bullshit, much? Like I said, until you get your ass somewhere where I can check on you, or you get back here; otherwise, I'm going to video chat you every day. Whenever I have a mind to."

"You're home then MJ?"

"No. I'm at the office. Then I have class in like an hour. Professor Derleth. It's the seminar on Occult Sciences that you overtallied for. We were supposed to take it together—"

"Listen to me for a second, MJ. Could you?"

"Where did you sleep last night? In the car?"

"You're not listening to me. You never do."

"Boo-fucking-hoo. What? I'm listening."

"There's a storm coming up the coast. I don't know if it's going to impact you up in Arkham. But, it's going to slam the shore here—"

"I didn't hear anything on the news."

"You won't. Probably not until the weekend. Don't ask how I know. Just keep an eye on the news, ok? If it looks bad, get out of the city for a few days. Don't come down here though. Here it's going to be bad."

"So why don't you just come home. Here home. The apartment home. I'll keep the room for you ok? You paid up until next month. I think I can pick up a few hours. Dr. Danforth needs to hire someone as a research assistant. More than just intern stuff around the office. She wants someone who'll go with her on cases. I was toying with the idea. It's not exactly my path, but I love working with her and—"

"You always do that, MJ. Get to the point. My breakfast is getting cold."

"Tetchy tetchy. Jeremiah, you're a whiney little bitch. Anyone ever tell you that?"

"Just you."

"My point, you dumb fuck. If she hires me, then I can handle the rent for a little while, as long as you're coming back. You have a think. Maybe I'll come to you for Thanksgiving and we can talk? Mom's going to be traveling, so she won't be in Salem. I think she's going to New Orleans or Paris or somewhere else, where she can forget this will be what, the eighth Thanksgiving without dad. You know she's been like that ever since she left Toms River. You're the only one I ever spend the holidays with. So, you think you'll be home by then— here home?"

"I don't know MJ. Maybe. Maybe, by then I'll come back to Arkham. I told you those people, the Allens, aren't my family."

"Yeah. I know, but you never answered me. Why go to Jersey then? And where are you going now?"

"To have my breakfast."

"Yeah, dick. After that. But why leave here at all?"

He shook his head, shrugging, but MJ couldn't see that. Jeremiah only appeared to her from the nose up. She shook her head at the idea that for all his smarts, all his know-how, Jeremiah was in so many ways a total luddite. He couldn't quite manage holding his phone properly. She saw more of the cafe shop window behind him than she saw of him. But, she was able to see the dark hollows beneath his eyes. He was a mess. She wondered if he had enough money to eat more than breakfast today.

"I don't know MJ. I think I'm going to check into a motel across the street. It's right here and I need a shower. I'm tired. I roughed it last night—"

"HA motherfucker. I told you. You look like shit. You slept where again?"

"In my car." Suddenly Jeremiah didn't want to tell her about sleeping at their old camp ground. He certainly wasn't telling her about the All-Father or the Marquis. "I'm going to get a room and hunker down for a few days while I decide."

"Why don't you just go back to the old house on Buchanan? Donna and Marvin are still there, right?"

He nodded and made an odd gurgling sound as he sipped his coffee.

"So go back there and figure out what's what. Don't waste your money on a hotel."

"I told you there's a storm coming. They don't give a fuck about me. Besides, they'll be evacuated by the end of the week. I might as well get a room now before there's none to be had."

"How the fuck do you know they'll be evacuated? Who are you, Nephren-Ka or something? What's going on Jer?"

"Nothing. I told you. I'm tired. Need a shower and a lie down. No worries about me MJBB." He hadn't called her that in a while. It was something he started calling her late in high school when he discovered her full name: Madisen Jane Brienne Berkana.

"Promise you'll text me when you're in the room and send me the name of the place. Room number, too? And no fucking dancing Mr. Beans. Talk to me. I want to know you're ok. Ok my brother-from-another-mother?"

"Yes." Jeremiah was filled with a love for exactly one person in the entire shithole of a world at that moment. MJ. He always did love her. There was only one time when he thought it was a different love than friends and she shut him down right quick. She said for all they knew his biological parents could be some relation of hers. She even joked that her dad had been a sperm donor when he was younger and maybe whoever Jeremiah's parents were, maybe they had used a fertility clinic and maybe they needed a sperm donor. Or maybe his mother was a single mom who used the same sperm bank which would have upped the odds that he was really her brother. They did become blood siblings during that blizzard back in '05. He smiled into the phone. "I'll text you in maybe an hour. Let me get there and get settled, k?"

"Ok. I'm calling you back otherwise. It's 9:45. I'm holding you to that. One hour. Love you *Jerry.*"

MARVIN & DONNA

"It was the very witching time of night...." Marvin laughed, squinting up at the sky which was heavily streaked with clouds like from one of his old comic books. He half expected to see a witch on her broomstick streak across the sky. *The Minturn Witch.* "All joking aside, Donna, what's going on here? Mrs. McGovern has always been your friend, even though I told you to steer clear of her. Old bat gives me the creeps. You never did listen. What you need me for?"

"When the Marquis calls, what am I supposed to do? Ask questions?" Donna walked up to the edge of the river, glanced around, was satisfied at how empty the block was, and produced a slender tube of glass from a padded pouch in her pocket. She needed Marvin to block the breeze enough so she could catch a light and take a few drags on her chillum before they continued on. She stood facing the river, wind blowing erratically as though a storm was heading in. *Something wicked this way comes* she laughed to herself inhaling, feeling her head lighten as she held. *Burnt offerings.*

The sweet diesel of OG Kush made Marvin's mouth water. He couldn't risk taking even the slightest whisper of a puff. Couldn't risk testing positive for THC so... he enjoyed the aroma while trying to stand upwind as they both faced the inlet on corner of Minturn and Bay Shore Drive. They had chosen walking the few blocks instead of drive. It was a nice night. Crisp. Autumn was his favorite time. He noticed, in spite the dim street lights that the water was unusually high. The moon was waxing gibbous and if the water was this high now, by full, it would flood the streets. Marvin buffed his nails across the front of his shirt, feeling a sparkle of conceit that he remembered his moon phases from junior year astronomy. *Yeah, suck it Marquis. Marvin Allen is the man.*

Still, he didn't know why he would need to be here. Donna had been the one working with the fishy old bastard. The Marquis. McGovern too. Marvin shrugged. Both were fishy fuckers and Donna's circle. Marvin really didn't go in for the whole alchemical approach. It wasn't his scene. He got enough blood and test tubes at work. Next solstice would be his tenth anniversary as an EMT in Toms River and he just wanted to get past this hump in whatever the master plan was. He needed a break but, like Donna said, when the Marquis said jump....

Marvin stood, taking in the sea breeze mingled with his wife's nightly medicine. The scents made him jones for a sweet lobster roll and a cold root beer. "So what's the deal, love of my life?" He glanced at his watch. It was way too late now. He supposed he'd have to wait for his lobster fix tomorrow— or get some lobster and make them himself. Most of the best places were already closed for the season. So, tomorrow it would have to be...

Exhaling slowly, savoring the smoke, Donna shrugged. "I can't tell you why he's here tonight. We were supposed to go across the river and meet tomorrow, nearer to the open water. I think it's near Asenath's time, but she's been saying she's near time for years now. I think the Marquis is tired of waiting for her to go. Be open-minded, ok? He has his reasons—"

"His reasons? Really, Donna? Light of my life, don't you see he's been jerking us around for, like, ever? We were promised things would be different for us. I don't have to remind you that my family has had a reputation for being, shall we say, gullible?"

"You mean stupid. The Allens have had more than a reputation, Marv—" Donna laughed. "What was Zadok, your great grandfather's uncle's cousin or something? Thirteen times removed, no less." She laughed harder. Maybe blazing up before tonight's meeting wasn't a good idea. Her toes started buzzing.

"Ha ha. He was my grandfather's brother. You know where his inability to ask questions got him. So, again I have to ask: why does the Marquis want us here, tonight? Wind's picking up and the water's rising. I'd rather be home rewatching 'The Angels Take Manhattan.'"

"Yeah for what the seventeenth time? Get over it. Amy's dead. Rory too. The Doctor's movin' on, lover. I'm telling you, I'm still not into Matt Smith as the Doctor. I'm glad it's his last season."

"You'd say that. Just remember how you fucking wept when Tennant left." Marvin screwed up his face. In a high falsetto, he whined, "I don't want to go."

Donna punched him in the arm. "Dick. You were crying too."

Marvin mimed pulling something out of his pocket, again with the falsetto, which he thought was a nice imitation of an English accent. It set Donna's teeth on edge. "Not bad for a man in his jim jams. Very Arthur Dent. ...what have I got in here? A satsuma?"

She punched him again. This time, lower down.

"Hey! Watch my satsumas!"

Chuckling to herself, Donna was grateful that her husband of the last thirteen years was into her geekdoms. They had met at an old *Star Trek* convention after all. They watched the same shows, read the same comics. The were the ones who introduced the kids to *Dungeons & Dragons* and until Jeremiah became a little asshat, they tried having family campaigns. But, she always found that despite the front Marvin put up, he never took to their adopted son. It was a burden the Marquis had laid on them that she never quite understood. Well, she did because of the kid's mother, but still. Donna wished there had been someone else in the vast Curwen, D'Bourget, and *Mason* line that would take the little bastard. She felt badly for thinking that about Kezzie's son.

Drag. Hold. Her head lightened considerably and she felt a little less badly upon exhaling.

Jeremiah's parents had had some position. Well, his mother did because of *who* Jeremiah's mother had been, a Mason after all. Donna thought it was funny. For all Jeremiah's genealogical sleuthing, his obsession with the Marquis, the D'Bourgets, and the grand Curwen line, the little misogynistic prick never once looked into his mother. She was the many times great grandaughter and namesake of Keziah Mason.

Kezzie and Donna had grown up together. They were sisters in all but name. Donna took another drag on her chillum, fondly remembering the two girls playing together with volume III of the *Diary of Samuel Pepys*. It stood in for their spellbook as they played in the sands off Mike's Island. They used to laugh, alternatively calling it Donna's Island or Kezzie's Island. It was their place and they loved spending summers there, just them, their mothers and the other women in the family. The girls learned how to draw the right signs, make the right potions, say the right devotions.

Then Kezzie moved away, back up north after her father had been offered up during the Nor'Easter of '96. The girls had just started their first semester together at Miskatonic, but Kezzie dropped out to spend more time with her family. When she came back to New Jersey, she had just married Josiah, a weird, slightly greasy guy from Chesuncook. Donna never liked him. Kezzie was already pregnant and she seemed more attached to the Marquis than to her husband. Wherever Kezzie was, the Marquis wasn't too far away. He was very fond of her and Donna had been a little jealous of the attentions her erstwhile sister had received from the Marquis. Jeremiah's father had been offered up himself, what was it, almost 20 years ago now? Not willingly of course, but he had to have some inclination as to his part. Himself from those weirdos in Maine. He never saw his son born. Donna always wondered if Jeremiah was truly that man's son...

Taking another drag, she realized she hadn't thought about Kezzie in some time. She missed the woman. Wished she had that old connection, wished she was surrounded again by her sisters, wondered if she wasn't wasting her life here in Toms River. Why shouldn't she go back up and be with her people? They were in New York now. She hoped this plan, whatever it was, would finally put an end to things here. The Marquis had his focus on Jeremiah and once things were settled, perhaps Donna could take her husband and go up north for a time. The kid was at school. He was an adult. He could make his own decisions now that he was of age. She had been patient all these years, but she was tired of having her life shunted this way and that. It was very hard being an Allen and even harder for a woman who wanted a posting of import with the Order. The Order seemed to look at her sideways, especially when they discovered her association with the Masons. Had she been blood to Kezzie, she never would have been accepted into the fold. The Order wasn't so traditional lately though, especially after they saw where tradition got them at Innsmouth. Donna took some comfort in how important Aunt Julia became in her own family line. Her mother's great aunt

Julia became the true Magna Mater, after all and cousin Jyssamin had done wonders with the family business. Ice cream, indeed. Donna's family, on her mother's side of course, was more coven inclined, but they were a nice marriage of the two paths. It made Donna angry that Jeremiah was so antithetical to her attempts to teach him— especially after he discovered his Curwen connections. She was more than qualified. But, the Marquis...

Marvin undertook getting his wife's attention, away from the twenty-yard-stare Kush always gave her. He started doing his version of the Silly Walk. She just smiled, eyes getting the stoner squint, and she shifted her focus away from the water to his antics.

Donna dragged, musing on the crackling from inside the chillum. She watched the glowing end and considered that for all his bluster, Marvin was perfectly happy being the errand boy. He did whatever he was told and he didn't ask why— and he was the one getting on her for the same? For not asking questions? It wasn't her relatives who had been offered up. Well, not the women at any rate. There were times she really did want to pummel him. She resolved not to go the way of the other Allens. Marvin didn't get why she wanted to position them close to the Marquis, despite her misgivings. The Marquis had become the head of the Order here and if Donna wanted her family to survive— and her family consisted of herself and her husband. Jeremiah was merely a veneer. He never belonged to either of them. He made that very clear, ever since he was a teenager. If that kid was the Marquis' focus, fine. She did what she was told.

She supposed being summoned tonight probably had more than a little to do with the facts.

Fact One: none of the Maxfield's ice cream she had liberally applied to Jeremiah's entire life, pretty much, did anything. No gills. No transformation. Nada. Come to that, it didn't have any affect on his friend, what's her name? Donna dragged again. Yeah, MJ. She was another anomaly. But, the Marquis had no concern over her. He said she was immune, which was unheard of in Donna's opinion. Whatever. Exhale and release...

Fact Two: the kid had been partaking of water spiked with essential saltes since he was what twelve? The Marquis had instructed her and Marvin to gather the saltes from all the offerings over the years. It didn't make sense, but the Marquis said it would be to prepare the child. To make him open. Righty-o. Hers was not to question why.

Fact Three: the kid got booted from Miskatonic, which was

the plan. Get his appetite whetted and when the spigot was turned off, it would make him more malleable. Fine. But she wanted this done.

Exhaling, Donna took a moment, stood the slender tube of glass upright on a nearby bench until the cherry stopped glowing. Replacing it in her pouch and pocket she popped a mint. "You wanna know what the Marquis wants? Let's go before they send out a search party, shall we?"

JEREMIAH

October 24th 2012 11:30pm

I got sidetracked and need to keep up with my journal. I have barely slept since I left the motel only this afternoon? I slept for a few hours and headed out while there was plenty of daylight.

But, I know now and have to log that knowing. The Marquis was associated with the Esoteric Order of Dagon. From having scoured my books and material, I now have no doubt of the origins of these fish symbols, manipulated as they appear from other similar sigils. They are a sign of the Deep Ones and Hybrids I believe are within the Toms River area. I'm already starting to see their signs.

I never suspected, in all my wanderings in Arkham, of the breadcrumbs I followed all over French Hill and the University District, both inside and outside the University, that there were Hybrids. I am shamed at how naive... what a simpleton I am!

What was the Marquis up to? My journey has become twofold. To discover more of the Marquis' disappearance and to implement some chaos magick upon the Allens. They're at the heart of this— of all my troubles. They have to be. Holding back my ancestry? Never sharing with me the situation around my parents death? Donna and Marvin always said their boat sank off Ortley Beach. It appears it's all inherently tied together. In being able to sense the long ancestral roots tied to these signs, each one becoming stronger now, pulling on my senses in ways I have never before experienced.

Okay, backtracking a bit.

I took a room at the Budget Inn, just across 70 from the Union Café. I slept for a bit, then packed my rucksack with all the essential go-bag accoutrement. I don't have a tent, but I packed a tarp, some paracord, a few emergency blankets, an emergency sleeping bag that makes me look and feel like a burrito. But it helps me keep warm. I've got my fire-kit, some tools, a first-aid kit, extra socks, tuna packets, granola bars. I remembered my collapsible packlite and a small roll of kitchen trash bags at the last minute. I figured when the storm hits, I've got to keep gear dry. My bag is water resistant, but I don't know how safe my documents or my ritual bag will be. I fished a large 2 gallon zip lock out of the back seat too when I remembered the packlite. The one MJ gave me after we tried an evening hike around Christchurch and I forgot to bring a flashlight. She found the neat little solar-powered lantern online and said since it strapped to the outside of your pack, it would charge as you walked. It's big enough to write by, so I'll be good for a while. I have a water filter, but I'm not in the Sahara. I'm heading down 37 and there will be places to get water probably every 50 feet. At least until the storm hits. Plus, I tossed in my journal, of course, along with my kit, my own book of shadows and my tools for the ritual I've been crafting. I believe now, if I conduct the ceremony with the Allens as the focal point, in the spot where the Marquis last stood, then perhaps I could connect to his energy and learn from my ancestor directly. Who knows, perhaps some of his essential saltes remain in the area. That would be the crème de la crème of this entire scenario. And, the fish-heads have been pointing me in this direction for years.

I paid at the motel through until November 1st. All Souls is a good date to aim for. Propitious. Auspicious and many things besides. The events of the next few days will point me to a rational conclusion....Or at least a conclusion for my current phase....Either that or I'll head back up north. Back to Arkham. So, I've got until November 1st to figure this all out.

I left the car with all my worldly possessions therein, and progressed east on Route 37 shortly after 4 in the afternoon. I walked for some time, heading toward the coast, taking my time, considering possible courses of action to focus my intent on the Allens when I saw another tentacled fish-head. This time upon a concrete monolith, barely visible from the road. At first, I thought it was another one glowing in my minds-eye. But it was there proper. High enough for me to spot it over the roadway in the trees maybe a thousand feet down from where I had stopped to catch my breath and drink some water. I was across from the Marquee Cinemas where MJ and I saw *Captain America* in 3D last summer, right before we left for Arkham.

I stopped right at the turn-in for the old Ciba-Geigy site. And, superfund or not, I was tired. I had been walking what seemed like all day. I considered ducking into the woods to set up camp. It would be the only stretch like this before the coast— and I really didn't want to keep walking down 37 in the dark. That's how people get killed.

I noticed the fish symbol as the dusk darkened. The sun was just going down as I saw this shimmer from the woods. The setting sun caught the symbol, flaring it golden for a moment, long enough to draw my eye. At night they have a silvery glow to them, just as bright as a solar powered lamp in the dark. At least they appear that way to me. I do not know if other occult practitioners in the area have seen them. I don't know if anyone else sees them. Maybe the Marquis would have...

I approached the monolith, realizing it was further off than I expected, just inside the treeline. Of course behind the fence. So I had to walk a ways off the road, out of the sightline of the security trailer, which looked like no one was home. Maybe a dozen yards into the trees, I found part of the chainlink fence was broken, bulging, loose enough for me to lift and shimmy through an opening I was able to make wider with the bolt cutters and crovel from my go-bag.

Approaching, I saw it now. A stone tower rather than one of the herculean monoliths from Mystic Isle and Seaside Heights. What was its purpose here? Inland? The tower stood about 20 feet high. Little more than 4 foot around at the base, it tapered to about a foot around at the peak, like a rounded, miniaturized version of Cleopatra's Needle. I placed my hand upon the cold material, and exhaled. It seemed to hold the cold night air. My finely tuned senses honed in on the symbol; looking up at it, I saw it truly had a phosphorescence. I closed my eyes. A cascade of energy flowed downward, chilling into my hand. An energy I have never experienced before coursed into me. I at once knew where all the tentacled fish-head symbols were located. The picture I received in my mind's eye was floating above the treeline. It was a trail of glowing symbols along Route 37. Knowing the geography of this area, I compared the image to the map of the area already in my mind. I had been pouring over Google Earth while at the Union Café, planning my route. I knew every feature from Crystal Lake to Vision

Beach. The symbols repeated, like breadcrumbs extending all the way to a structure just off the Route 37 Bridge to Seaside Heights. Pelican Island. It had the runes from my dream scrawled on the mental map. The Marquis' last known location.

It was empowering, but I was left more than a tad tired. As the energy poured into me, filling me with a glowing sense of purpose, I felt a pulling, a sucking that I could almost hear as the opposite to that mental whooshing of the universe settling into place. My ears popped as though the barometric pressure shifted. My eyes dropped and I started to nod out, there with my hand still on the preternaturally cold stone.

I wished for a home to head to so I could sleep, but I managed to pull my hand from the stone. I was deep enough in the woods, away from Route 37 and Disney Drive. How appropriate to name a road, literally in the midst of the nation's most toxic site, Disney. Great. And I'm sleeping here tonight. Brilliant.

I strung up my tarp between two trees. Cleared the ground, and started building a quick bed. There would be no fire tonight, sandwiched where I was between the site and a housing development. I also knew the turnoff from 37 was often monitored by police seeking to fill their quotas. It wouldn't do to build a fire. I was able to shield my packlite and spent some time reviewing the ritual I've cobbled together, before updating my journal. I suppose now I'll hunker down for a bit. I've made a nice little nest with a few layers of branches and emergency blankets. The cold is settling in as the wind picks up... Snuggling down in my emergency burrito sounds good about now. How about a few more hours sleep?

BULLETIN
HURRICANE SANDY ADVISORY NUMBER............12
NWS NATIONAL HURRICANE CENTER MIAMI FL.....AL182012
500 AM EDT THU OCT 25 2012

...CATEGORY TWO HURRICANE SANDY PREPARING TO MOVE OFF THE NORTHEASTERN COAST OF CUBA...

THE TROPICAL STORM WARNING ALONG THE FLORIDA EAST COAST HAS BEEN EXTENDED NORTHWARD....
INTERESTS ELSEWHERE ALONG THE SOUTHEASTERN COAST OF THE UNITED STATES SHOULD MONITOR THE PROGRESS OF SANDY.

MJ & JEREMIAH

"Slow down, Jeremiah. You're not making sense. And stop moving. I can barely hear you with the wind, ok? Plus you're huffing and puffing. I feel like a broken record but, where'd you sleep last night?"

"I told you. I camped by the old Geigy site. In the woods—"

"Fuck Jer! I thought you were glowing. Isn't that radioactive or something?"

Jeremiah stopped walking. He looked like he was in a parking lot. He had just walked up a road, then had pushed his way through a thicket of trees, and finally had walked down to a building that she recognized now as the Walmart on 37. What did he do, sleep behind Walmart? Why the fuck—

"It doesn't matter MJ. I've been heading toward the coast—"

"Why not come home? You said there's a storm and there is one heading up the coast. I don't think it's a big deal. I mean Irene wasn't as bad as they were all saying, so this one won't be so bad."

"MJ you're doing it again. I called you this time. Stop rambling and listen to me. They're here."

"Don't tell me you've been watching snowy channels again. *They're heeere.* Should I call you Carol-Anne now?" She started giggling. Jeremiah knew MJ enough to know that when she laughed like that she was nervous.

"I saw the sign again, this morning. I was woken up by it. I was in the woods just across from the Marquee on 37. I told you that. I had packed up camp and was heading along the treeline, thinking I'd start walking a bit down there instead of head back to the highway. I liked the quiet. I was coming out of the woods and a fucking van almost plowed me down. Fucker had one of the symbols on the side, inside the company logo. Looked like some repair truck."

"What'd it say?"

"Sounded like the Deep Ones tongue, or a disease. Berge Hvacr. And beside the B and the ending R there was the fucking fish-head. I've been telling you, but you haven't been listening to me."

Jeremiah's voice piqued. She wasn't sure what he was up to and wondered idly if she shouldn't talk with Dr. Danforth. She was driving to the office now and MJ didn't want to jeopardize getting a position with the woman, but Jeremiah was on a downward spiral. Though, MJ might consider speaking with the Allens first. Then he could get some help and she wouldn't have to worry about fucking up a job before she had it secured. Her foot was barely in the door and it had the potential to be her career. She loved Jeremiah, but would she give up her livelihood because he intended to go on some solo LARP?

"Ok. So you followed a truck, did you?"

"I did more than fucking follow it. I wanted to know exactly what was going on and how many of them were in Toms River."

"Them? There's a them now, Jer?" He was delusional. Had to be. This wasn't good. Mrs. Allen was getting a call.

"I told you. I've been on their trail for a while. The symbols. They've led me here. Now I see that there *are* Hybrids in New Jersey. I spoke with them just now."

"And what did they say?"

"Nothing. One wasn't even in the vehicle. He was on a house-call or something."

"So we have Deep One repairmen at the Jersey Shore?" MJ would have laughed, if it wasn't Jeremiah. She did enroll in the abnormal psych class, at Dr. Danforth's behest. The doctor said understanding normal human psychosis would be essential in their work. It would help them determine markers and better link up the dots on an investigation, identify susceptible individuals, possible insights into motives and all that. So far, Jeremiah's behavior was raising more than a few red flags. Had he been a subject instead of a friend, MJ would have absolutely gotten him into some sort of hospital or observational program. She might have to take a leave and go get him, storm or no storm.

"Have you been listening? Seriously MJ. Your eyeballs get that fucking glazed over thing when you're there but not there. My arm is getting tired—"

"I've told you before, relax your arm. It's a phone not a fucking umbrella. And don't get pissy with me, Jeremiah. I heard you. Berge Hvacr. A truck on a house-call with the symbol you kept seeing at school on the truck's logo. Let me clue you in, though Jeremiah before you get your panties in a bunge. Hvacr isn't a Deep Ones conspiracy. H-V-A-C-R stands for Heating, Ventilation, Air Conditioning *Repair*. Hello. Repair truck. And, let me tell you something before you continue to pitch a fit in the fucking parking lot of Walmart. You are scaring me. You get a caution at school and are told to take the term off to get your shit together. Instead, I come home from work to find you cleaned out your fucking room. Left me a note. I didn't get in your grille about that. I let you have your moment. But, I figured you'd be going home. You didn't. You're squatting in the woods, on some pilgrimage to the coast, during a storm no less, and now you're telling me there are Deep One Hybrids working as AC repairmen?"

"Well, when you put it that way, it sounds nuts. But, yeah. I spoke with the guy. He had the fucking rash. The scaling skin. His eyes were black and he spoke with a lisp that made him gurgle like he couldn't stand the air. I mean, I'm not nuts, MJ. I told you this is where I need to be. I've got to finish this thing and see what the Marquis was up to. I also know now that the Allens have been screwing with me. For all I know, they killed my parents."

"What's this now?" MJ couldn't believe her ears. Her phone was safely cradled on the dashboard mount otherwise she would have dropped it. Taking her eyes off the road to glance at him quickly, MJ saw a grey cast to Jeremiah's face that she hadn't seen earlier. He had done what she had asked: keep her updated on his whereabouts and his doings. But, unlike yesterday, he had called her. For the last, what week or so since he left school? Two? She was getting old. Losing track of time. She had been the one who called him. Usually in the morning just as she was getting to class or to the office. Today, she was driving back from an overnight at Jaimie's and her mind was rehearsing the interview. Even though she had been interning with Dr. Danforth for several months, since last Spring, the Director of the Armitage Research Division still needed to play by the rules and subject any possible hires to an interview of the board. Today was not a day she needed Jeremiah's shit, but she felt a bit guilty that her friend was in crisis and she was obsessing over her career. Jaimie told her as much last night. She took a breath deciding to pull over to talk to him properly. She pulled onto the shoulder on Sentinel, right at the corner of Washington Street, in sight of Christchurch. She didn't believe in premonitions, not really, despite her work with The Estimable Doctor Nora Jean Pym Danforth. But, staring at the cemetery gate, MJ was truly frightened for her friend. "Tell me what you're talking about Jeremiah. I'm sorry. I have an interview in an hour and you're right. I wasn't paying attention. I've pulled over. Tell me what's happening."

"I have been. The Allens are behind my being booted from school—"

"But—" MJ bit down on the inside of her lip. She had to control herself. She was sure, if Jeremiah was having some mental disturbance, that to him it did seem like he had been kicked out of school. Especially after the letter from Mrs. Allen to the College Board. Between that and what happened with Dr. Danforth... She breathed and listened to him.

"I told you all this already, before I left. I am certain that my parents didn't die in any boat wreck. I couldn't find any evidence of anyone disappearing off Ortley Beach, but that's besides the point."

MJ did find that after her own father died, she was more understanding of Jeremiah's predicament. No matter how wonderful she thought the Allens were – funny, patient, approachable. Shit, Mrs. Allen was the one who gave her her first DM manual and taught MJ how to make her first herbal remedy: Ginger-lemon tea with elderberry. It was MJ's go-to remedy for colds and it got her through her first winter in Arkham. But, Jeremiah was right. The Allens never talked about his parents, beyond reminding him at every turn that they took him in. But, the idea that they orchestrated his parents' demise? That was nuts.

"I'm not getting into the particulars. But, I saw the truck and spoke with the one who waited for his partner. Of course he pretended like he had no fucking clue. Like he was just any corporeal with zero understanding of this stuff. But, I know what's what. I'm onto them and I'm not stopping now. This has made it more imperative that I get to Pelican Island before the storm hits. So, MJ, if you'll forgive me, I have to go. I'm sorry I bothered you before your interview." Jeremiah's tone dropped to normal levels. "I'm going into Walmart to use the facilities and get something to eat—"

"In Walmart? Go get something decent at Pisces or Hooks or something."

"I'm walking MJ. I told you that. The car is back on 70. If the storm hits, I can't lose my car in any flood. Everything is in it. I'm on foot."

"I thought you were joking about your pilgrimage."

"You should know me by now." He shook his head. He truly was alone in all this. The Marquis had to be his savior. He couldn't rely on MJ any longer. Time to wear the big-boy pants. "I'll call you tomorrow. I have to conserve battery power—"

"Can't you grab a bite and plug it in while we talk?" She suddenly didn't want to let him off the phone. She felt if she didn't keep him talking, she might lose him. A panic rose in her chest and she felt she couldn't breathe. She'd have to reschedule the interview. She started a mental list of things she'd need to grab for the drive to Toms River. Pelican Island. It wasn't too big. She'd be able to find him if she drove around the shore for a bit. Especially... if he didn't answer his phone.

"Don't come down here MJ. I told you. They'll be evacuating in the next day or so. I will be fine. I will come home after I'm done here. Ok?"

"You're listening to my thoughts are you now?" That was coincidence. Synchronicity is what Dr. Danforth called it. But it made the back of her neck prickle.

"I'm going inside now. As you said: you can't jeopardize what could wind up being your career for me. I'll be fine. I'll call you in the next day or so."

Before MJ could say another word, Jeremiah ended the call. She sat staring at the cemetery gate through the trees and she felt sick. She turned on the radio, scanning for a weather update somewhere. She had time to head home for a shower before the interview. She settled on telling Dr. Danforth about Jeremiah after the interview. He was right...She couldn't abandon her goals and yet she couldn't ignore that he was going through something bizarre, even if it was only a mental break and not a Deep One invasion. But, Dr. Danforth would give her some assistance. She hoped.

NEW JERSEY TODAY WITH MIKE SCHNEIDER FOR OCTOBER 26TH 2012

"Today Hurricane Sandy takes aim at the Garden State. No one in their lifetime has seen a storm like this. Governor Christie prepares for the worst. There's already been some evacuations down in Cape May.

"Hello, we begin tonight with a deadly serious situation. Hurricane Sandy has already killed at least 39 people, rampaging through the Caribbean, pummeling the Bahamas, and moving further north into the Atlantic towards us, where a rendezvous with a cold weather system could make this a monster storm...."

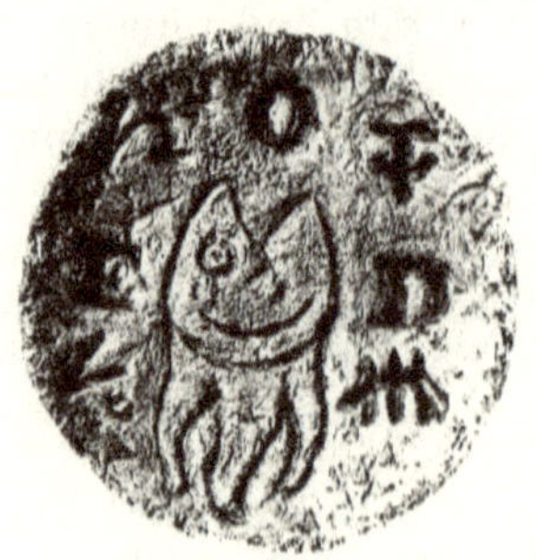

JEREMIAH

October 26th 10:23pm

I'm about ready. The waves are lapping the shores nearby and the sky is an ungodly green, almost like a tornado is brewing. The moon is near full and despite the growing storm, I can see quite well. But I have my lamp regardless. I will be brief. I have little time before my first attempt at the ritual.

I've shut off my phone. After the last bickering with MJ, at her reception to the idea of Hybrids here, at her rebuke of the idea that yes the Aliens killed my parents! I cannot speak with her. I must have my mind clear. I must set to work. The words have filled my mind and I can hear Him calling me— all of them. The Marquis. Me. The All-Father.

I was far from satisfied at my interaction with the Berge Hvacr agents yesterday. I found two more of their vehicles between yesterday morning and earlier today. I followed the last one just blocks from the old house. It stopped right at the corner of Minturn and Bay Shore Drive. The driver wasn't the same one I had questioned yesterday, but he went right up to the door of the old Minturn Witch! How could this not be happening? And like this?

I didn't want to stay there, in case Donna or Marvin turned up. So, instead of investigate, despite the 'roadmap' already shown to me back at the Geigy campsite, I headed across the Route 37 Bridge, heading east toward Seaside Heights. As I walked, mindful of the wind tearing off the water, which seemed to rise, slightly but perceptibly as I trudged along, I thought about the mental map. There were two blips here on Pelican Island. Two symbols. One was as bright as the monolith at the campsite. The other was barely visible, but lay somewhere ahead, just off the bridge.

Most of the way across, it was fine. Traffic was heading the opposite direction since a partial evacuation order is in effect. It's voluntary, but a lot of folks were heading west. There were a few hairy stretches and I almost got mowed down by that garish home décor place, right at the head of Pelican Island, by a red-pick up as it sped around a dawdling motorist. Fucker tore off down the shoulder, almost taking my legs off as I vaulted over the short fence where the yard of Shore House Coastal Decor began. The sandy lot, usually covered with an assortment of sea-themed outdoor bric-à-brac, was empty. I crashed onto the sand, landing awkwardly on my leg. I couldn't move for a minute and was convinced I had broken something. I was enraged at the idea that some peon, some unskilled clueless corporeal would prevent me from doing what I needed to do! I howled at the red pick-up as it disappeared down the road.

The sand beneath me was streaked with pink. I realized my leg had a pretty nasty gouge across the knee and upper thigh where my pants had torn. I must've cut myself on a bit of stone or shell embedded in the sand. In my daze, I thought I should take some for later. The blood on the sand might be useful. But, I didn't have time. There were a few fellows who had been setting about covering the windows with plywood. They saw what had happened and came over at a rather quick pace. I didn't think it proper to tell them to wait while I scooped up a specimen of my own blood on the sand. But, I silently offered it up to the All-Father as the two men approached.

I noticed one had a certain shamble to his gait as though there was something wrong with his feet, but he still moved as quickly as the other. One of his hands was malformed. The fingers seemed fused almost like someone with a thalidomide birth defect. It looked like a flipper and he used it like any regular hand, along with the other guy, to help me to my feet. It was fortuitous because as they took me inside the shop, I noted the fish-head symbol drawn in chalk, like I had often seen in Arkham, drawn beside the shop door. The flippered man saw me eyeballing the sign and smiled. He said nothing. His companion mimed that Mr. Flippers was a mute. The two were kind and helped me bandage my leg. They gave me a chipped mug of hot tea that tasted like someone had washed their socks in the tea kettle. But I was grateful for the warmth. Walking across the bridge had chilled me. They invited me to stay for something to eat, but I couldn't stay there in the back room of the shop. I took a few moments rest, sipping at the tea and listening to the weather updates on a small black and white television the men had in what looked like a small break room for the shopkeepers. I hadn't seen a black and white television in years. It easily looked to be my own age. After hearing what had to be the seventeenth talking head note how "Sandy was the storm of the century", I determined on leaving the shelter and the clichés, thanked the men, and started to head out to complete my task.

"Try the north cove, over on Sunset North. There's a little spot looking over Harbor Island. Most of the block left by now. You might have some luck out there. If not, head across to the beach and try this address. You're not far off now." The man patted my hand as though we shared some joke as Mr. Flippers was scribbling something on a small card.

I tried not to recoil at the touch of his misshapen hand. Aside from the awkwardness of his walk and his hand, there was nothing remarkable about his face. Nor his companion. They couldn't possibly be Hybrids, could they?

The card bore two addresses in a peculiar, childlike scrawl.

"This is here. North cove. Houses are empty. I wouldn't try getting in though, security cameras and all that." He laughed as he pointed at the card. "If that doesn't suit, try here. You can get a meal there too. Provided they haven't left yet. But, I don't think old Marinus would close shop unless the National Guard forces him to. You should know by now, Jeremiah, the storm doesn't bother us. This is what we were bred for."

So no, they weren't corporeal; they were Hybrids. I didn't

question him. I should have, but after drinking the tea, my mind felt lighter, free from the burdens of quizzical thought. My chattering brain had ceased as the pain in my leg quieted.

"Marinus runs the bar over on Carteret. Make sure you go in the back way. You might not find your way in through the front."

I didn't know what he meant. But, again. I didn't ask. I nodded. Thanked him and started walking across Pelican Island. My going was slowed by my leg, which began to throb as I neared the first location: 201 Sunset Drive North.

There were a number of empty houses along the road, and a few whose owners were finishing their preparations before heading out. No one paid me any mind. They were focused on the impending Sandy and I was invisible. I didn't find anything suitable, however, along the little dribs and drabs of beach. The afternoon waned as I approached the address. Looking across the cove to Harbor Island, I wondered if it was more suitable for the ritual than here on Pelican. Despite the lore, I didn't feel a pull from any part of this place. There wasn't anything here....Could the Marquis have been held across the cove at Harbor instead of here on Pelican Island? Maybe. I had seen the map in my mind back at my campsite off Route 37, but I had assumed the symbol here was Pelican Island. The chalk drawing at the décor shop had to be the dim one I had seen on that mental map, but what about the other one? I hadn't been drawn to any other place on Pelican Island. So...where now?

As I stood there, I noted a small boat landing behind the house, maybe fifty yards away. I headed down the small strip between the houses, toward the single boat bobbing at the dock, instead of the house itself. As I considered my options, the afternoon sun dropping behind me, I saw the familiar glint of the setting sun catching fire to one of the fish symbols. It had to be another monolithic needle, like back at the Geigy site. There was my route.

The small craft was a single engine boat that had seen better days. I stepped into the vessel, and with an intention, yanked on the starter, hit the clutch, and it was ready to go. I untied the boat from its mooring and steered it out of the narrow channel and toward the shimmer on Harbor Island. As the wind worsened, the waves chopped in a see-saw motion, which made my empty stomach roil. I remembered the sour tea from Mr. Flippers and tried not to vomit over the side. I tried not to question my rate of survival just to get to the area I needed to be in.

As I steered the boat my mind raced at the encounter I had had. Between the two men at the décor shop and the Berge Hvacr agents? As questions arose in my mind, the shore of Harbor Island loomed darkly before me and to my right floated by what appeared to be tiles and chunks of coral. Something was happening. Had the storm already hit buildings along the coast nearby? I didn't think so. I hadn't been listening much to the news, except snippets that had been on the television in shops I had stopped in, for water, and at the décor shop.

After a few near misses with varied debris, I steered the boat toward the shore as the wind did most of the work, pushing me toward it. The steep shore came upon me rather quickly and the boat crashed against a short, rocky bit of beach, throwing me forward, almost off the vessel. I had managed to steer up to the island, just past a sand bar easily three-times the length of the boat. Had I not been guided by the forces clearly at play, I would have grounded the vessel some distance off shore, which would not have boded well. I stood, gained my balance, and jumped out of the boat into two feet of water. I managed to tie off the boat to an odd stone piling jutting from the beach. It looked like an old jetty. A few yards into the trees, I noted a stone wall and a path heading inland. I negotiated climbing onto the old wharf, being mindful of my leg, and looked around for the symbol I knew was here. I could see it barely visible just inside the treeline.

It was another monolith. It looked out onto an expanse of rocky beach which faced Seaside Heights. I saw the edges of sandy beach-line near Route 35 across the water. But this tower was taller and wider than the one by the Geigy site. Another needle, but it had a more rounded top, like a cross between a minaret and the domed onions topping St. Basil's in Moscow. I placed my hand on its cold exterior. As before, images surfaced in my mind. No roadmap. I saw the gallows on shore and a silver noose swinging on a summer morning, the sun barely out of its bed. This was the spot where the Marquis had been. I heard two voices whispering in a tongue I did not understand. One seemed to be female, while the other was undoubtedly the All-Father. The two voices mingled, one louder throatier, a deeper gurgling I had yet comprehend. Was this the language of the Deep Ones? I must learn it I told myself. Then I heard the me-yet-to-be shout: *Brujo!*

There were several hours to moonrise, so I set up camp. There was some stone structure, like a two-sided breakfront, sticking up from the small strip of sand, between the needle and the shore. It would be perfect to shield any fire from prying eyes across the cove. I readied myself while I made my fire, and, in preparation for the first attempt, I've emptied my mind into my journal to document this all.

The moon is steadily rising before me and I shall begin.

Per Adonai Elohim, Adonai Jehovah, Adonai Sabaoth, Metraton On Agla Mathon, verbum pythonicum, mysterium salamandrae...

October 27th time unknown; daytime. Maybe an hour before noon?

I woke by the water lapping my face. I was about five yards away from my camp, face-down on the shoreline. I had been dreaming of a grand alchemical past. I saw creatures twisting from a maelstrom of butterfly wings with fractal animals, insects, flowers, and sea-creatures all diving, dancing, twirling into a symmetry that I couldn't hope to describe. As I observed the discourse of the dream, I heard a voice. Distant at first, but it came nearer. I realized the dream was being narrated by Terrence McKenna. He spoke in a sing-song voice of an alchemical monarchy and the need to recapture my past by looking to my future, a bifurcated universe one degree out of sync with normal consciousness, a mirror held at a forty-five degree angle to eternity. He spoke about a counterpoint of time versus space versus future, which is the past, which is the cosmic heartbeat and the breath and the brainwaves of Gaia.

He began rhyming something I think might have been the song Frodo sang in the Prancing Pony, right before he went slap through the floor...

"The man in the moon took another mug and rolled beneath his chair. And there he dozed and dreamed of ale until in the sky the stars were pale and dawn was in the air."

But he said it in a way, though rhyming, like it was the most advanced, most magnanimous proclamation anyone had ever made. And yet he reminded me of Professor Greene telling me to keep my mind on my studies. He murmured about the mind of the All-Mother and I wanted to correct him.

Isn't it the All-Father?

As the sky melted, he began shouting in Shakespearean tones about constipated nitwits and their blood-sucking stooges.

Then his rhyming went back to singing as though he hadn't started yelling into the fiber of my brain. His voice cleared and the sky blossomed into a thick mucus of black sludge, rimmed with a rainbow sheen, like oil-stained water. It dripped down, congealing into a spheroid that pulsated before me. The voice was a chanting that reminded me of the Yule roundels Donna's ladies choir would sing. The same phrase repeated, grew, crescendoed and other voices, all McKenna's in various cadences looped into the melody, creating a vast, counterpoint polyphony:

"Per Adonai Elohim, Adonai Jehovah, Adonai Sabaoth, Metraton On Agla Adonai Mathon, verbum pythonicum, mysterium salamandrae, conventus sylvorum, antra gnomorum, daemonia Coeli Gad, Almousin, Gibor, Jehosua, Evam, Zariatnatmik, veni, veni, veni. Per Adonai Elohim, Adonai Jehovah...."

The song continued while he told me to separate the dross from the subtle matter, to preserve the essence, to rarify and to grow and to transmute... I realized he had been singing my spell, which had failed. Nothing had happened. No flashes of light. No sound of the agitation of the fabric of nature. My spell wasn't met with a fury. Not even a fart. I was horrified. I was the cosmic, constipated nitwit. The stooge. I fucked up.

McKenna began to sing again, but this time he sang the address on the card Mr. Flippers' companion gave me. And then the voice became the All-Father. It was McKenna and it was Dagon and it was the me-yet-to-be. Then the voice became flesh before He was consumed by what I can only describe as one of MJ's Gelatinous Cubes. It was the jet black pulsating spheroid with a veined surface... hideous, a viscous protoplasmic mass with iridescent eyes... I heard the voice extending past the undulating surface of the creature as it absorbed Him, McKenna's eyeballs, sparkling with phosphorescence, floated on a surface that spread, vast, like the sea. Churning, expanding outward. His voice was extinguished as my eyes opened.

I thought I was being devoured by one of those blobby things, that my eyeballs would be disgorged to float on the gelatinous surface, alongside the disembodied eyeballs of Terrence McKenna.

But it was the sand and the water. The tide will cover this place soon. I need to leave. But I wanted to document that dream before I forgot.

The sky tells me it'll rain anytime and the winds are steadily increasing. I can't mull over this much more. Not here. I don't think my ceremony did much, except give me a sore throat and psychedelic dreams.

The storm hasn't even hit yet. I'm not sure what I was thinking. The moon wasn't even full! How overzealous. How stupid.

I've packed up my gear and I got everything in plastic. I feel like a bag lady, but as long as my important stuff stays dry, I'm fine. I'm heading for that last symbol. I can assume it will coincide with the second address. It must. This might be the last journal I can log for a while. Who knows. I'm getting back to shore while I can still manage the boat.

FRANKENSTORM REACHES THE JERSEY SHORE

"So what's the status of our Frankenstorm, Lee?"

"Thanks Liz. I'm standing here, at the corner of Bay Shore Drive near Coates Point. Seaside Heights is across the bay behind me there. Right there, is the now closed Thomas A. Mathis Bridge. Governor Christie has closed all bridges statewide, as have Governors Cuomo and Malloy. As you also heard earlier today, President Obama discussed possible emergency declarations across the Mid-Atlantic States."

"So who will be impacted by this storm, Lee?"

"Honestly, Bill, anyone east of the Mississippi. Hundreds of thousands have already been evacuated tonight. And we've already learned that schools will be closed for over 2 million children across 7 states and Washington D.C."

"Mandatory evacuations are in place for low-lying areas. Tune to ABC7ny.com to check your zone and find a shelter. But, what's the deal with this, what is it, a fujiwhara effect?"

"Right Liz. The fujiwhara effect is when the vortices of two storms, with their cyclonic action merge to make a superstorm. Looking pictures from, NASA it's clear this is storm is a leviathan at over 1000 miles across. And long before it makes landfall, sometime tomorrow night, it's already being felt all up the coast, with whipping winds and rains which have already flooded many communities up the coastline. I just have to mention that the clouds stretch from the Carolinas all the way to Hudson Bay and really spike North almost to the Arctic Circle. This is an impressive, incredible cloud canopy. It is one of the largest, if not the largest storm we've seen in the Atlantic Hurricane basin. Between the winds, the predicted rainfall, and the full moon? This is truly a monster storm."

DONNA

There is something happening that Donna couldn't put her finger on. Besides the damned storm. She wished Marvin wouldn't stay glued to the television. He finished boarding up the windows, finally, yesterday, right when the evacuations started. But they hadn't upped things to mandatory levels, yet. She was certain they would any day now. She was finishing her own preparations while she had to keep reminding Marvin to get this important or that important thing out of the basement and upstairs.

For all that she loved him, Marvin was not the swiftest egg in the basket, as her mother used to say. When she was a kid, she'd laugh at the idea of an egg being fast, but when she was older she thought her mother wasn't talking about chicken eggs... but something else. She shuddered. She had to give him a bit of a break though. The moment they had returned from that bloody mess of a meeting with the Marquis, they started preparing. Marvin had taken a few days personal time. He knew once things got real, once they declared an emergency, he'd be called in to do back-to-back shifts. Until then, he would be taking care of the heavy lifting. Literally, lifting all their machines on cinder blocks and trying to see what was irreplaceable and what could be offered up, all that *plus* making a massive store run for supplies, non-perishables, plywood, and whatever else they thought they'd need. Clerks at Home Depot and Shop Rite laughed, calling them both Judgment Day preppers. *Let's*

*see where they are in a day or two if they haven't started preparing
yet.*

She doubts either of them slept after Minturn. They were at
the store the moment it opened the next day, but they had already
started moving things around that night, right after they had gotten
home. They figured the washer, dryer, and fridge would all be a loss.
But, Marvin set about pulling all their bookshelves upstairs, after he
had already pulled box after box of books up as well. Not everything
went up, but anything with sentiment. They were happy they didn't
have much in the way of collectibles, a few, but the books and his
autograph collection went into the attic. He laughed and was pretty
pleased with himself for using the assorted book boxes as a base for
their foam mattress.

The one thing Donna had obsessively hoarded was cardboard
boxes. The moment she determined that Jeremiah was not open to
being her son, not truly her child, her protege despite his being of the
wrong gender to teach properly, she secretly wanted out. She
promised herself as soon as their task was done, they'd go back up
north. So they would need moving boxes. Half the attic was full of
them all flattened in bundles. She also had cases and cases of packing
tape. Any time so much as a roll was on sale, she'd snatch it up. They
both had been working pretty much non-stop for more than two full
days. Inside and outside. They also wondered what they'd do with the
car. But, then she remembered, he'd take it to work and Community
was high enough above the flood zone. She hoped. The two of them
had no generator though; besides, she didn't want the headache. So,
they'd go it old school and have a camp out in the attic. There
wouldn't be much of a need to light the camp stove, she hoped. But,
even so, the skylight should be enough to get any fumes out. She did
regret not going to that survival tracker school thing with Marvin all
those years ago. It might've given her another level of comfort.

Especially since she'd be riding out the storm alone. He
would be at work. Well, she'd have the kitties as company, but still,
she didn't think Mr. Flibble and Sméagol would fend off the storm.
They might help her in her own workings though. Help figure out
what else was going on.

After they tackled the store and before he started on the
books, his meager collectibles, and the assorted antiques she didn't
want to lose if she could help it, her Jensen-style chest and cabinet
were of prime importance. She'd have the set airlifted onto a
mountain if she could. Marvin simply put it at the highest point in
the house: on the raised dais on the north wall of the attic. This was
an odd feature that she now utterly appreciated, because it would

raise the chest about two feet higher than the rest of the attic. The top would still clear the rafter-ceiling by about a good foot. Plenty of room for her mother's books. The 17th century marvel chest-cabinet duo, with its oak foundation, it's olivewood oyster-cut veneers, its princesswood seaweed marquetry, was commissioned by Margaret Dee, daughter of the man himself. It was a true family heirloom. Margaret Dee had no children of her own and she commissioned it to celebrate the birth of her grand niece, Jane Pomfret, the matriarch of Donna's maternal line. Donna was sure the chest was a true Jensen with all it's intricate designs. It had been passed down ever since and it was the storage house of all Donna's tools, her herbs, and her grimoire. It too had been passed along, matrilineally, all the way back to Margaret Dee.

Miskatonic never taught those secrets of Dee's family. The once-male only school with their still mostly male faculty always thought Dee's son Arthur inherited his father's skills. When that fell to the women— and there were plenty of them, starting with the three Dee sisters: Margaret, Frances, and Madinia. Donna's namesake. Donna Madinia Waite-Maxfield.

She would not lose her family heritage because of some little storm.

It was Donna' own cabinet of curiosities and Marvin had wanted to leave it there, in her work room, which was adjacent to their bedroom. But, the Marquis had warned them to get their proverbial ducks in a row. The storm would be Dagon-raising shit. Although, he didn't grant permission for them to evacuate. Donna wasn't surprised, but she didn't feel the pull to leave. Not yet.

Marvin was in need of a rest though. She took a few more moments, watching him as he sat flipping between ABC and CNN. Though if she heard Blizter's beard utter the word Frankenstorm again, she would freak. Marvin was taking a break on the couch, sandwiched between the their pride: two Maine Coons. Donna had their carriers and litter boxes already set up. Marvin's shoulder almost gave out as he had humped the Jensen upstairs earlier and he needed bit of a siesta. Luckily the upper cabinet separated from the lower chest of drawers so Marvin was able to handle it himself. Still, he was pushing beyond his limits. She knew that. Her too.

She had spent a portion of the day after the confab with the Marquis emptying the entire cabinet, top and bottom while Marvin made room in the attic for just about everything, including the Jensen. They both hoped the water wouldn't reach that high. But they also both remembered the images from Katrina, of people clinging to rooftops. While Donna had worked—wrapping, boxing, and transporting all her tools, her jars, curios, and herbs— she knew she needed to clear a space wider than the cabinet though, to keep a place for workings clear. So arm's length around, at the very least. The weird raised platform, where she and Kezzie used play theater while girls, would probably be sufficient, though she'd have to make sure she didn't twist an ankle or fall off while she did her casting. She decided, even though she would need to bring the cabinet back downstairs at some point, she would pack everything for a long-stay in storage. So she was especially careful with the most vital and delicate pieces. She might not be seeing them any time soon. She also dug out her old Mary Poppins valise, one she used for overnight stays with her cousins when she was younger, and created a kit bag to keep with her if they really had to go-go. She pictured Peter Vincent Vampire Killer and tried to smile. She would be the spook by night, though.

And all because of the Marquis. All those offerings for him and his interests instead of for her and hers? She hated herself at that moment. Why hadn't she been more discerning? What the *fuck* had she been thinking? *Mother would be ashamed.* ...Especially after Minturn Avenue the other night? After the way the Marquis sat at Asenath's own table, glaring with his dead shark eyes, his bulbous mouth rimmed with what was clearly blood? Without a trace of Asenath McGovern anywhere. The Marquis claimed she had gone to sea with the rising tide.

There was no way possible that Tante would leave without Donna to sing her home. Had Donna brought any tools, she might have challenged him herself. But, she knew she wasn't a match. He was almost 300 years old. This was still Donna's first lifetime. She would only be 45 in a month or so. Asenath herself wasn't even 100 and if she couldn't handle him, how could Donna?

But that wasn't it. There was something else. Something brewing alongside the storm. Donna intended on surviving this thing and taking her husband out of here. She wouldn't allow either of them to be offered up— not for the Order.

She tried. For Marvin. For the sake of her father's memory. But, this was no longer her path.

She needed to get Marvin moving again. He'd have to finish helping her bring the frozen containers up from the deep freeze to pack in the kitchen fridge, as well as bring the canned stuff to the attic. She had three apple-crates full of her canning jars, chock full of the new stuff on the kitchen table. She was also canning a pot of refrigerator soup. Everything perishable– all the wonderful veg they had gotten at the farm only last week, the day before the Marquis' convocation *in Asenath's kitchen!* Donna had already washed, chopped, and merged into a chutney, peach-apple barbecue sauce (after the apple butter failed), and a pepper relish. She was happy the day of the confab, she had already prepped the fruit. The farm trip was precisely to get the end-of-season fruit and make her chutneys, relishes, and apple butter. Everything else they picked up in addition had become a mammoth minestrone chittering happily in the pressure canner. All her canned food supply, the majority of which she home-canned herself, were also nestled into a corner of the attic. Marvin had already filled a bookshelf with jars alongside the cans of Honeyville freeze-dried stuff that she had forgotten at the top of the pantry.

She was pleased neither she nor Marvin had ever had hoarding tendencies. Well, besides their ginormous food supply. She was sure they could live for at least two months, maybe three, without having to head out for food. Their attic was at best a third full. She thought there would be plenty of space for their valuables, and themselves, to ride out the storm. Marvin had also stocked up on water, opting for more than a few 5 gallon jugs on top of the cases they routinely kept on hand. He was never a survivalist, but he always wanted extra bottled water on hand. They both did, not having much confidence in New Jersey's aquifers. Especially after all the contamination from that fucking Ciba-Geigy site? Contamination which extended to Fort Dix? All those girls in Toms River and Dover Township coming down with cancer, from what? Had to be the fucking water, Marvin said. She didn't disagree. She was happy they had easily 10 cases of water, plus as many gallons, on top of whatever he bought at the store early this morning. He just had to hump them upstairs.

She made an effort to rescue anything she thought might have been important to Jeremiah, but she wasn't sure he'd be coming back anytime soon. If at all. She hoped, as she told her husband, the kid would stay in Arkham. Her survival and her husband's would have to take precedence over anything of that kid's— Kezzie's son or no.

But, there were those dreams last night. And this heaviness in her chest— and the Marquis had fucking blood on his mouth!

Enough daydreaming, Donna! She actually slapped herself hard enough that Marvin looked up past Lee Goldberg and with his pink button-down, over Mr. Flibble's silver-tufted ears.

"Hon?" Marvin twisted away from the tele, craning his neck to look at her. "You ok?"

"Yeah. Just woolgathering. I'm just about done in the kitchen. You're finished with everything else, are you?"

"No. Just taking a rest. Christie might close the bridges and there's already a stink that Bloomie isn't cancelling the city's marathon. He wants to see how bad the storm is before he shoots down the city's chance at raking in millions. Little Napoleonic shit wouldn't care if Staten Island was washed away, as long as the New York City marathon could go on. Not sure which is worse— the blimp or the midget. Shitheads."

Donna nodded and headed into the kitchen to check on the pressure canner. She couldn't help but wonder, Marvin's diatribe notwithstanding, if Jeremiah was involved. She would need to ponder and prepare. Once everything else for the day was done. Another task to add to the list. All she had to do was get them to Halloween and then, she'd see about heading back to Arkham herself. Jyssamin did have a standing offer to visit. Donna was certain a change of scene would be much needed. Just survive somehow.

JEREMIAH

October 31st 2012 6:45pm

My bones ache. I feel older. I have a healthy stubble going and when I saw myself in the mirror, I noticed a lot of silver peppering my face. My hair has started growing again. The motel has running water, but brown. Still. It was enough to wash the grit, the slime of the storm's foul floodwaters from my skin. It was truly providential that I left the car here. No electricity. Brown water. Confusion everywhere. Nonetheless, it's like an oasis amidst a war zone. I'm writing this with my trusty solar-lantern and trying to get this down before I crash again.

I suppose the chaos might have been of my doing. That's what I get for casting chaos magicks. But, it was supposed to be focused on the Allens. Not all of the Tristate Area. I can almost hear MJ snickering in my mind: *And you think you're responsible for Superstorm Sandy? Jerry you ponce.*

I did make the attempt. Twice. And I do have the tablet now. So... it stands to reason... that whatever intent was within the storm, I may have amplified....

I should be ashamed, especially seeing the devastation I've thrust upon my neighbors.

Why should I care though? What support, what succor have they given me? Why shouldn't I unleash hell itself on everyone? The corporeals. The Allens. Danforth and the entire board of Miskatonic University.

But then why not focus it back on them? Why here?

It's like the tantrum I had with MJ the night her father died...

I think I'm beyond mudras to calm myself. So, I'll go backwards for a moment, to focus and strengthen my recall. Didn't Jonathan Harker have Mina do the same: track, catalogue, record every instance in order to discover the patterns?

Ok. So, I found my way back to the motel earlier today. I was picked up, maybe yesterday afternoon? So, Tuesday afternoon. By Coast Guard. Taken to a local shelter where I was gawked at incessantly. No one believed I could have possibly survived the storm on the shore, let alone at Seaside Heights mere blocks from where the Jet-Star was swept out to sea. So, I stopped saying that's what happened. Even though I saw the roller coaster rising from the water, skeletal fingers of a great sea beast aborted... and it had to be what, four or five stories high? The monolith where I rode out the storm was as high, perhaps higher, but it was in its own fold in time. Like McKenna said. We live in a bifurcated universe which keeps refracting, undulating, folding in on itself.

I managed to find a crack. Maybe the crack was opened from my efforts at Harbor Island.

I can't think of another explanation. I survived. Intact. And so did the tablet. But, their city is destroyed and perhaps all this was some predestination to remedy that? Fractured but still...

I slept at the shelter until this morning and I managed a ride to the motel. Between the boat trip to the shelter and the journey here, it was like a tornado tore up the roots of the earth. Boats tossed in the middle of roadways. Cars floating in canals. Devastation and a low wailing, of sirens, of generators, of mourning echoing in my ears.

I thank Dagon and yes, the All-Mother too, the Magna Mater was there in the mouth of the storm and She let me go.

I'm not sure the All-Father would have. Not if He wanted me there with Him. The Magna Mater... one I never put much credence in... until now. She rejected me. Cast me aside. Perhaps She prevented me from succeeding?

Why would She protect the Allens? She didn't protect the rest of Jersey. Or Her own city if that indeed what added to the melange in Sandy's floodwaters.

Going backwards again.

After Harbor Island, I hazarded the boat on the water and made it to shore, docking just by Stewart's Drive-In, by Route 35. That had to be the 28th? No. It was the day before. The 27th. The roads were packed with people heading to the mainland. I did attract the attention of a police cruiser as I dashed across Route 35 and Bay Boulevard. He pulled over and I half expected him to follow me as I crossed toward the elementary school on Kearney. I needed a place to hunker down.

I had the address on Mr. Flippers' card: 65 Carteret Avenue. I could picture it in my mind so I kept my head down and tried walking between the houses instead of on the road. It took a lot longer, weaving my way up Kearney and across to Carteret, evading stragglers, police, and what had to be the National Guard. I didn't think they had been called up, but there were a few soldiers helping board up shops and homes. I almost got stuck in the alley between the Thunderbird Motel and another derelict motel next door. Literally stuck in the narrow space, but I took off my pack and shimmied through sideways, twisting my injured knee again. Hooray. I popped out like a cork, scraped but whole. I eventually found myself standing at 65 Carteret.

From the look of the building the impression the average person would have is that it was abandoned and forgotten. I knew better. This was one of those folds in space. Sort of like Diagon Alley, I supposed. Outwardly, the building was unremarkable. The outside patio was broken cement. The door seemed high, but unremarkable, like the rest of the building. Nonetheless, it reminded me, with its pillars, like a cross-between St. Mark's Church in Warren, Rhode Island, a bit like East Church in Arkham, and your standard Masonic Temple.

The building could be seen. So it wasn't entirely like Diagon Alley. The corporeals had to see something. But, its luster was secreted away in that fold of space-time. Though, on each level— outward and inward— it was sorely in need of a little TLC. It must have been a glory in its heyday. A once majestic front door— glass papered over, dark wood, cracked and weather-stained oak or walnut — was easily twice my height and seemed wide enough to let in a team of horses, four abreast. Or a Deep One?

Over the door, a half-moon of glorious scroll-work sat. It looked like the sun on the horizon with what I thought were rays twisting outward. I realized they were tentacles rising from the ocean to envelop what had to be a setting sun. I was certain the glass door might have once held stained or bevelled glass instead of a hodgepodge of newspaper and peeling masking tape over cracked or missing panes.

I scanned the area noticing every crack and crevice. How old was this building exactly? It appeared to have repairs from before the turn of the 19th century. Missing were many of the wooden roof tiles, which reminded me of the type you'd expect to see atop a Norse mead hall. The siding too... only to be sealed with bad patch jobs. The wooden awning was caving in, though it was supported by worn cement pillars of a moderate size. But, inwardly, I saw another dim fish-symbol. Not in chalk like at the home décor shop, but it was on one of these pillars: a small carving of the tentacled fish, which I stretched up to touch. Just as I reached for the door, out of the corner of my eye, I saw part of the paper covering the inside of the glass on the door shift and a single large eye blinked at me.

I heard in my mind more than with my ears. "Prepare yourself first. We'll come for you."

It was but a matter of seconds as the eye and I made contact and the paper shifted again, folding back into position. The eye was gone. This was an odd encounter to say the least. My stomach rumbled and I realized I could not remember the last time I ate anything. I also realized I couldn't recall exactly what day it was. Prepare myself first? My stomach made a valiant effort to eat my spine and I suppose a meal should be part of any preparations.

Immediately next door was a sports bar that seemed not to have gotten the evacuation notice. I had already walked past it without truly seeing it, I suppose. I walked back toward Boulevard and came to the front of Hooks Bar & Grill. I thought I could risk a meal before heading back to what I could only imagine was a Hybrid Temple. It was only next door and they said they would come for me? I shrugged, reading the handwritten sign out front. A chalkboard read: "F*!k you Sandy! Fridge Clear-out specials! Drinks half off! Cash Only Before we LEAVE!"

I reached for the door as it cracked open about a foot almost making contact with my head. A couple exiting, one of whom muttered as they passed by, in a whispery, gurgling angry voice: "Go the fuck away!"

Me? Was this a Deep One hideout? I went inside, intent on either finding out or feeding my belly before it ate me alive. Inside was a normal bar, lots of wood, some half-hearted attempt at a nautical theme. There were maybe two other patrons and a skeleton crew preparing the place for the impending storm.

"Grill's off, guy. Got sammies, sliders, maybe some disco fries à la Chef Mike. No ice though. We're closing in about an hour, so get while the gettin's good."

I nodded at the barman and took a seat at the far-end of the bar, ordered sliders and the fries with a simple bottle of water. About midway into my meal, which was served up inside of the 10 minutes it took to plate and zap everything in the microwave –chef Mike indeed— I ordered a sandwich for later. I asked the barman to wrap it well so it wouldn't get wet.

"You riding out the storm here? That wouldn't be advisable. Evac is mandatory. Island is shutting down by the afternoon. Once the bridge is cleared, it's closed. Gotta get out today, man. Don't make people like my brother risk his life because you want to stay and watch your shit, man."

I bit back several retorts, wanted to tell the burly, neckless wonder to mind his own business. That he, a fucking earthbound mundane corporeal, couldn't speak to me: Jeremiah Allen D'Bourget Curwen in such a manner. That I had been guided by ancient spirits to find this place and no infantile thing like an evacuation order would cease me in my quest.

I simply nodded. Thanked him for his concern and told him I would be meeting with my uncle, that we would be leaving shortly.

"Who's the extra sammie for, guy?"

Before I could respond, a hand clapped down on my shoulder. A flippered hand. It wasn't Mr. Flippers because a brusque voice said,

"He's with us, James."

"Figured as much. Who was in charge back there anyway? You know we're leaving. I won't make any suggestions. Your French frog fucker won't listen. Don't tell him I said that. Whatever. Sammie'll be ready in two." He went back to the kitchen. Could I have been mistaken? Was he a Hybrid too?

I was torn from my seat by a harder grip on the back of my jacket, and it forcefully pulled me to my feet. I noticed the man had one hand. Well, one visible hand which ended in an appendage again like a thalidomide flipper. The other hand was hidden in Napoleonic fashion inside the front of his coat, which was stereotypically a peacoat that had seen better days. It was worn, patched, and had mismatching buttons. He seemed to be far older than the two men who had helped me at the décor shop, but his voice was younger, deeper. It had a growl rather than a gurgle. If it wasn't for the flipper, he reminded me of Quint from *Jaws,* but with a snug watchcap covering a head seemingly devoid of hair, except a few greasy strands. His face was bearded, but it was so sparse it seemed like he had rolled his grey, scaly skin in goose feathers. Had I seen him before my meal, I would have been put off.

He yanked me by the back of my jacket to a door down a corridor at the back of the bar that I had previously thought was a restroom. The door was thrown open and I was pushed through with the new, gruff, evil-smelling Mr. Flippers shunting me behind. The door was slammed shut behind us and he propelled me forward, thrusting something rigid into my back, knocking the wind out of me. It was dark and my sight was not adjusting properly. I was pushed against something flat. The door?

After a few heartbeats I heard a gurgling, phlegmy voice near me say, "He does not smell like Zadok."

My heart stuttered when I felt and heard something sniffing quite close to me. Does he know my foster parents? I had become aware of the Allen ancestry as I eventually had done some research into it, but only after I had first looked into my own biological family. Only in the weeks before I got the boot from Miskatonic, did I learn the role the real Zadok Allen played. Were these creatures before me and the ones I had met at the décor shop the same Deep Ones, or Hybrids, that had sacrificed Zadok? My chest tightened with a slight onsetting panic. I felt that abysmal, roller-coaster about to move feeling that I often do when I've smoked too much weed.

Another deep sniff, the feeling of what I initially thought were stubbly whiskers upon my forehead, and a sour pickled smell made me regret having had a meal à la Chef Mike.

"No, he is of a mixed bloodline, that of the Marquis and that sorcerous Curwen.... but...I smell something Other." More sniffing. I could barely see my hand before my face. The dim light was blotted out by a squat form bending over me like a fat Grim Reaper but with catfish like tendrils which skittered across my face. I stood transfixed, my soul being devoured. I sensed it was tasting my ancestry. "Mason! He's a MASON!" The catfish-reaper Hybrid scuttled backward and again I felt a jab, this time in my side.

The voice near me was interrupted by a louder, throatier, deeper gurgling I hadn't yet heard, a voice I couldn't comprehend. There were clicks and pauses along with a litany of gurgling. I wondered if there weren't notes too high or too low for human hearing. Was this the language of the Deep Ones?

I must learn it I told myself, again.

Another hard jab in my side, then the flippered appendage holding me against the wall, or door, released. I was shoved forward, yet again, and driven down what I expect was a corridor of some kind. I couldn't imagine it extending that far toward the back of the building. Hooks was a large bar, but I had already been sitting toward what I thought was the back when the sinister Mr. Flippers had pushed me through that first door.

But, perhaps this was another crack. Another bifurcation in space-time.

My eyes adjusted, slowly, but steadily. I had been heaved into another bar. This time, instead of the light, spacious, honey-colored sports bar with its sickening array of flatscreens littering its walls, this bar was heavy. The air thick, the wood black tarnished with time and grease. The worn wooden bar was more than shoulder high. It was impossible to sit at without a high stool. Were the Hybrids giants? But my escorts weren't much taller than I am. Looking up, crudely carved into the paneling behind the slick, begrimed bar was the tentacled fish-head, this time adorned with a coronet and runic symbols that were beyond my comprehension.

I was turned so that my gaze was being guided. As I was positioned, I saw what had jabbed me in the back only a few short moments earlier. Sinister Flippers didn't have a Napoleonic mien. He had a fucking claw large enough to decapitate and it had been stuck in between my shoulder-blades. But, I couldn't react. My gaze was itself compelled forward.

Facing me was the silhouette of another reaper-like figure. Stalwart, possibly overweight, head shrouded in a large hood, which was suddenly turned down. Something glistened in the sparse light, a golden twinkle, upon it's head.

Was that a crown of gold?

The deep gurgling voice I had heard earlier in the corridor had come from this being in front of me. Yet, he addressed me in English. I was barely three feet from him and the smell was unbearable, a combination of spoiled fish, salt water, and feces.

It reminded me of the jug "Uncle Zadok" had forced me to drink from back at Crystal Lake.

As the unblinking bulbous eyes looked upon me, I felt dozens of slivers, slicing into me, as if daggers had been cast. *Tsentsak*. The black darts of the brujo. *Virotes*. The first volley froze me, heightening the crawling, tightening sensation in my chest. I hadn't been prepared for this.

What did I think, though? That I would be accepted with open arms? Swept into the warm embrace of a teacher, a father? What did I expect, Dumbledore?

If the second volley didn't cause me to stand rigidly, my knees would have collapsed beneath me. My leg and upper thigh burned. I mutely hoped I didn't have an infection, which was the least concern at the moment. I could hear the wind battering the outside of the building and I wondered idly if we weren't separated from the sports bar. The Hybrid Temple? I could not see anything as a third volley attacked my eyeballs.

This was not the way of my ancestors. In all my gleanings from my research, from my musings and wanderings, aided by Danforth's truffles, I believed that my ancestors stood up to the unknown. I imagined that this was why the Marquis had disappeared.

But, where did I think the brujo fit in? Not merely a male magic user, a brujo on the path of the plant medicines I had studied, meant one thing: the eater of souls. The sorcerer who wanted to sow discord, to harm rather than heal. I knew this. I thought I would somehow be put on the path to expand my abilities, to learn how to hone my own skills as brujo. It was a path I fully embraced, but I didn't think it would be turned against *me*.

An intense guttural sound agitated the air. Was that a laugh?

"I...am of the belief we are already acquainted..," came a slow susurrus in my mind. It left a disarray, scattering behind it. I was unable to focus to defend myself. "Do not fret rabbit, I know what you seek. You could say I am here for you to know the whole story before you tread off to destroy your adopted family..."

"Wha...what do you mean, who are you?"

"For all your investigative talents you have not figured out what is transpiring here? The rabbit does not know it is being pursued. Or does it?" Again the chortling which reverberated inside my skull. "Oh, yes, the documents illustrating my research into Yha-nthlei....the Deep Ones... their temples... have yet to make it across your desk, though you've tried to find more. You did well to follow the breadcrumbs here. That was always the intention. To keep shunting you along. We pulled you hither and thither across Arkham. But anything of true import has been well hidden beyond your limited senses...."

This was him. The Marquis D'Bourget. I had imagined him to be a sorcerer not unlike Joseph Curwen. I don't suppose it ever occurred to me that the Marquis I had sought was a Deep One Hybrid?

"I see your mind. We will one day perhaps become one... I can confirm that at one time the Marquis occupied the same flesh as this one."

The dim light seemed to come from the diadem-wearing fish-head above the bar and the Marquis' own crown; they shone with a phosphorescence reminiscent of my dreams. They were at once dimmer than the tentacled fish-heads I had been following, yet brighter on an internal level. They made an afterimage that seemed to glow, expand, brighten across my internal vision. It gave me the same disorientation that a camera-flash would to a person long since in the dark. I could see, yet not.

The Marquis' bulging, shark eyes widened, his obese fish-head glittered with pocks, scattered deep scars, whorling in the patterns of some unknowable tribal initiation... shambled closer.

"Yes, I see it...the recognition of my blood mixed with your own...You are more a D'Bourget than a Curwen, my progeny. Welcome Home."

Then, one of the others interrupted in a clacking, clicking in their language, punctuated with the imperceptible tones. The only word I could discern hissed and slithered about the room: Mason.

I felt the virotes lessen as my neck and throat momentarily slackened.

Regardless of all the occult lore I have learned, family history, spells, and alchemies, I felt a scream which had been welling up within me, a primal long held scream that I was finally able to project loudly into the face of the long lost Marquis D'Bourget.

This came as unexpectedly as this word Mason. What were they talking about? Freemason? I didn't understand. This isn't what I had signed on for. Had I been mislead? Had the All-Father lied? And what about the me-yet-to-be? Were my dreams a sham?

Was MJ right? Was I losing my mind? Maybe I should have gone back home... to Sentinel Street....

After a few seconds of my continued scream, Sinister Mr. Flippers clocked me with his claw and I remembered he could snip my head off without warning. The other clapped what I now saw were webbed hands over my face. I quieted, but was by no means calm. The virotes attacking my eyes also contracted and I was able to finally see the Marquis. He was as I saw him in my dream, standing behind the All-Father. He seemed to be a version of the All-Father. Instead of emerald green, the frill upon his head appeared as old armor, greyish-green that had its own luminescence in the dim light. His face was scaled. The neck extending down into a robe of undetermined color – dark, but not exactly black – was the pale underbelly of a frog. His hands were hidden in the sleeves of his robe.

Or MJ's Sahuagin. The Marquis gave me the creeps. He was no Curwen. No man. He was indeed a blasphemous fish-frog of nameless design — living and horrible.

"We have known of your presence in Toms River, as you have had an idea of our own. However, this Mason connection has not occurred to us. We eradicated the Waite Harridan. Your mother has been useful but perhaps she hid this from us—"

The almost imperceptible mumbling, clicking, gurgling again. The webbed hands relaxed across my face, but the claw clapped down on my shoulder painfully.

"Perhaps you shall lay waste to the Allens. Maybe they have surpassed their usefulness. We knew before Zadok's sacrifice that he would be the progenitor of lowly pawns. We knew the Harridan's connections to the termagant, the Maxfield harpy...we knew naught of Mason....Now the Allen foulness? Their half-breed descendants occupying the space here, in our town, must be wiped clean."

He clicked something in their language and Mr. Webby came forward like a boy scout waiting for his merit badge. I thought I detected a smile on his catfish-reaper face. That sound must have been his name. The Marquis continued: "...will show you the way. You were right. We are inside a space apart from the hackneyed humans beyond, the corporeals as you deem them." He waved a hand that was as webbed as his Hybrid boy scout. "You will stay here tonight only. Time is swifter on our side of the... crack, did you call it? Yes," again the shuddering, reverberating sound that I felt in my bowels. Laughter. I vividly hoped the mythical brown note was just that— a fiction. But with this third laugh, I felt a loosening in my midsection. So not cool. He continued, a definite smile playing on his frog-face. I suppose that might be the shit smell permeating this place. Had he laughed the crap literally out of people? Before doing what with them?

"Cease your ramblings." Again Mr. Webby's incomprehensible name. "—will show you to a room. You will sleep. Time does not move as you are accustomed. He will take you to where you will conduct your ritual when it is time. I believe you know the location. With the document I shall give you, make your magick and find your way back to us. You shall be sheltered from the storm.... Long have you been prepared, the road is not finished yet. I see this within you" His stare was unwavering, but he did not throw more virotes at me. I felt the few remaining withdraw slowly, excruciatingly. "Do not make the mistake of not returning, or it shall be your last."

He bowed his head and then a final virote shot from his webbed hand. "Sleep."

I can only assume I must have collapsed. I have no recollection of what happened next, or for some time afterwards. My next memory was standing outside, on the sidewalk of Carteret, on the cracked patio just in front of the Hybrid Temple. The door was open behind me as though I had just exited and Mr. Webby began shuffling outside beside me. The Marquis remained inside but within arm's reach. He held up a bundle I recognized as my journal, my grimoire, my papers from my rucksack, which I had thought was where it was supposed to be. *In the bag on my back.*

Did he have my ritual bag too? I wanted to snatch it from his hands, but I remembered his tsentsak.... I had no wish to repeat *that*.

From the folds of his robe he produced a parchment scroll, which he shoved in my hand. Was this my bonus spell of transmutation?

"You have no need of your toys. All you need is on the document. Get on now. [click-glubber] will show you where you will wait. Your toys and your papers will be safe. You will find them when you return to your car. Go."

I was launched from the building by an unknown agency, not unlike the virotes. It shot out in a wave, but did not affect Mr. Webby who stood a few feet off, his catfish-reaper face undulating like seaweed in a tidal pool. Creeps indeed.

I followed a mere two blocks down Boulevard, wondering all along about the time and the day. I felt like Frodo in Lothlórien. Time moved differently in a bifurcation in space-time. I shouldn't be surprised.

The storm wasn't here, not yet, not fully, but the winds tore down Boulevard, sending debris and the occasional sign whipping by. The rains were due to fall any moment and the sun seemed absent from a sky the same shade as the Marquis' gray-green frill. It was the tornado color I had seen from Harbor Island.

Mr. Webby stopped at the corner of Hiering and I came to an astonished understanding as I was faced with the monolith from my dreams. It was the same monolith MJ's father had been killed on....where most of his dismembered remains had been found. Yet, it was also the same monolith where the me-yet-to-be would stand, where the All-Father would rise.

How was I not aware the two were the same before now? Because, as with the Hybrid Temple, there was a shifting, a separating of reality and two monoliths appeared. One unremarkable in that it was much the same as those further south in Mystic Isle: what appeared to be a single cement slab. Outwardly, it was maybe two stories high. No higher than the sports bar.

Inwardly the surrounding area was dwarfed in its shadow. It stood, vast, but it was not a single block of cement. It was in the fashion of the Cyclopean walls of Ancient Krani, in Greece. We learned about it in the class. Learned about the power held in the angled, but tightly fitting sides. Being faced with a great wall of these impressive, rough-hewn boulders, I too thought they had been shaped by giants. Rimming the entire structure in a spiral pattern was a monstrous staircase. Set into the stairs, which had no railing, were twisting serpentine shapes.

Mr. Webby pointed up, and said not a word as he shoved me forward. He did not cross Hiering to the monolith's side of the street. I nodded and proceeded ahead while he returned back from whence he came.

The pall from the monolith mingled with the roiling clouds. A gale tossed me past the curb and into the fist step of the mountainous staircase, itself of a prodigious size. It was a herculean effort –from the size, to the intent behind it, to the struggle to climb it. As the wind increased, I dearly hoped each flight would not take such energy to mount. I had to heave myself up, pull myself over, and cling there while the wind tried to tear me from the edifice. As I ascended, the tempest accelerated. This is what the hobbits felt like on the steps of Cirith Ungol.

I had no choice but to take the stairs upward.

As I neared the top, it seemed like days later, the rains started. The sky remained the gray-green color it had been earlier. It couldn't have been much past noon, though I still couldn't catch sight of the sun. There were three steps remaining. I mustered what seemed like the last of my strength and pulled myself up, arms shaking with the undertaking. At the top, I was met with a familiar sight: the tentacled fish-head.

This time, it emanated from an ancient stone that seemed to yawn above me. It was a structure, like a doorway, but with a crazed look. Between the stone – itself covered over with a frenzied network of interlacing lines, almost like the streaking on marble – and the insane angles, this was the product of a diseased brain. Instead of holding myself there, legs dangling over the abyss, waiting for the gales to lift me skyward like some deranged kite, I slid forward onto my belly and rolled onto my back. The gateway menaced above me.

I could see the fish-head on the lintel. This time a lot stronger than ones I had previously encountered. I found myself compelled toward the stone. I did not have any control, like with the Marquis' virotes. But, my legs shook and I could not immediately get to my feet. So I crawled, back on my belly, snakelike until I was beneath the arch. It wasn't more than eight or nine feet deep, though it seemed like it was a hundred feet high. I couldn't help but think of those damnable saints on the half-shell which littered the front lawns seemingly everywhere. But wrong. Colossal.

I continued to crawl forward, and once past the threshold, into the three-sided chamber beyond which looked out to the ocean, the winds abruptly ceased. As did the rain. I was able to sit up, on an intricate spiraled floor, laced over with more serpentine designs, and in a few moments, stand. An immediate vertigo made me crash to the ground again, landing on the central image of what appeared to be a large coin perhaps a yard across. It bore the tentacled fish-head surrounded by the letters EOD and the runes I recognized from my dream: from the paper I held and from the tattoo the me-yet-to-be had on his back.

I heard a voice in my mind tell me to rest, replenish, remain. I crawled to the far wall of the structure, removed my backpack, and leaned heavily against the wall. Appreciating the solid stone beneath my back. I dug around in my bag and found it had been emptied of almost all my gear, except for a knife, my first-aid kit, several bottles of water, a vicious yellow something not immediately recognizable, and the extra sandwich I had ordered at the bar. I fell on it as though I hadn't eaten in years. While devouring what had to be the best sandwich in the history of forever, I recognized the yellow something. An inflatable life-vest.

The me-yet-to-be wasn't wearing one in the dream. I wondered if it was advisable to don it before I began. I wondered if I would know when to begin. I wanted to sleep.

So I did. I must have, after finishing the sandwich and a bottle of water. I think I may have tried urinating off the side of the monolith, but that might have been another dream. Then, after a time I can only assume I had slept –or sat in a narcoleptic stupor— as with the Marquis' virotes, I sat upright, my body rigid, lifting unnaturally to my feet. I began moving without thought or intention. The victim of an unseen puppet-master.

I donned the life-vest and before I buckled it in place, I pulled the scroll the Marquis had handed me out of my deep, inside, jacket pocket. In the realization I was being controlled— yet again— I found myself gripping each side of the parchment scroll quite tightly. I centered myself, grounded with my breath-work regimen, hoping I could lessen this supernatural hold through a concentration of will. I looked upon the document, deep rhythmic, slow circular breaths. Calmer, more in control. Yet the decision to continue felt more mutual than singular, as if the dominating energy agreed.

Upon the corner of the page was the Deep One's tentacled fish-head sigil, which reminded me to look upon the stone beneath my feet. What was this place? Was this where the Marquis had gone before he was taken to the Deep One city? He must've received his transformation there. He was too advanced to have accomplished that on land without tapping into the Deep Ones' power source.

But what was this, the central disc? As I stood on it, widening my stance, grasping the parchment, an aura, a vibration from this stone, coursed through me and I turned my attention back toward the document. The wind was loud as freight train tearing around the archway I still stood beneath. I was inside an offshoot of a branch from our regular space-time. Hurricane Sandy's fingers couldn't catch me here.

Now was the time. Before me the sky was a twist of black, grey-green, and white, waves against the sides of the monolith. I daren't look down or move, or the spell would not be complete.

The language was in the abhorrent, croaking tongue of the Deep Ones, as once described by Robert Olmstead. The parchment consisted of odd linguistic symbols that had to be a Deep One alphabet, and below each line was a translation in English, multi-syllabic words I have never seen but somehow recognized. My mind focused its intent. Reading each word, at such a quickened pace, I was again receiving supernatural guidance. My unseen puppet-master shepherded me on, in the recitation of each word.

Midway in my reading, glancing up, I saw three tidal cones rise from the waves. I half expected the spires from my dream. No. These were the reason for the gray-green sky. Waterspouts. Tornadoes of the sea. In the pandemonium, pieces of the same coral tile I had seen off Harbor Island, were washing across the top of the monolith. I peered down quickly and saw I had been standing in several inches of water. Panic wormed up from my belly and threatened to strangle the words in my throat.

I looked back upon the paper, which was now quite damp, yet the ink did not run. I had stepped beyond the archway, but I did not recall moving outward. Glancing down again, I could see the tremendous coin still beneath my feet. Perhaps it moved. Not me.

Raising my hand, focusing my energy toward the tornadoes shining blackly against the lengthening night, I read the last portion of the arcane ritual, the tornadoes sprung away as quickly as they had formed. I believed they leapt on their way to the Allen household.

As the tornadoes fled, the parchment scroll tore from my hands. I foundered trying to grab at it, landing on my knees and falling face down in the water. I'm surprised I wasn't tossed out to sea. But I was permitted to half swim, half wade back to what I hoped was the shelter of the archway. The fold in the universe was calm and free of water. Since the words and the scroll left, along with the waterspouts, I have not felt the presence of any controlling energies. Perhaps they were specific to the ceremony and not the Marquis' darts? The winds screamed around the archway and I hunkered back against the far wall to wait out the storm.

I had to have fallen asleep. I did not recall doing so, but it was like back at the Hybrid Temple. I had missing time. Perhaps time sprinted ahead here, as with the Marquis. One moment I watched the black tempest, keening around me, the waves rising impossibly, yet held at bay by whatever force kept the archway safe. I could feel the stone behind my back shimmy and I wondered if a single block shifted, would the protective bubble burst?

Then, I was waking to distant warning sirens signaling to anyone or someone specific out in the Bay. I got to my feet, stretching slightly. As I moved toward the threshold, still not wanting to cross it since the water refracted clearly against the invisible barrier, two things stared me in the face. The glow of the stone coin where the ritual was performed was back inside the alcove with me. And there was debris all over the floor. Coral tiles all glittering with a phosphoresce, littered the ground, etched and painted over with serpentine designs, much like the ones here at the monolith. But, here and there were images of creatures, not unlike the All-Father's priests and priestesses from my dream. Was this from the remains of a structure devoured by the storm?

No. Large pieces of flotsam were masonry, whole arches, pieces of columns, the occasional hunk of stone similar in style to the cyclopean blocks of this monolith, though not as humungous. There were a few piles of the stuff near the stone coin, I looked toward the threshold where a mound of tiles were glowing brighter than the ones further back. Stooping, I began digging in the pile of strange, broken, tiles, slicing my hand cleanly across the palm as I came to the source of the light.

A piece that was not exactly coral, but of a material I was not at all familiar with. Wave after wave crashed against the barrier before me, so close I could reach it with my fingers. I was certain if I had, the bubble would truly burst, and with a force that would shatter me against the far wall of this otherworldly grotto in its own slipstream in time.

I grasped what was a stone shape, roughly nine inches across and five to six inches wide. It was facedown, but I knew it was something of considerable power. I held it in both hands, the surface slick with my blood, which the stone seemed to absorb. Turning it over... Recognition. It was the herald-shaped tablet from the mouth of the All-Father Himself! The images represented were beyond comprehension. The border displayed what I recognized as the language of the Deep Ones. A few of the letters I recognized from the Marquis' scroll. Without the guidance of the spell, I could not possibly pronounce any of it now.

Indeed, I must study their language if I have any intention to use the gift of Father Dagon.

Within the borders of the tablet, I could recognize the strange barrel-shaped creature that was unrecognizable in my dream. An Elder Thing. And that meant, the preponderance of eyes and teeth? I had to believe belonged to a Shoggoth. How could I not have recognized either from my dream? They littered my Miskatonic textbooks, as well as the Marquis and Crane documents I had nearly memorized stretching back to those first few I had gotten from Orne in 2005.

I clutched The Elder Tablet close to my chest like it was a baby and I tried to run toward the back of the alcove again, to ride out the remainder of the storm. But, I couldn't move. I felt the waves shudder against the barrier and my ears popped. The presence within my head returned wanting me to head back to the Deep One bar where I had obtained the ritual document. But, something else was happening. A war which caught me in its web. I managed to shove the tablet inside my jacket, zipper it closed, rebuckle the life-vest, and pull the inflation cord just as a titanic wave smashed in, rupturing the barrier.

I could do nothing to fight the war which agitated me back and forth. I felt like I was trapped in the death roll of an alligator.

This all brings me back to now. So much for crashing again. I've been writing for hours, but I'm not as tired as I was when I began. My stomach roared, but there wasn't much help for that. Not now.

Since I'm writing, it can be assumed that the Marquis was correct. When I found my way back to the motel, my papers, my journal, my ritual bag, everything the Marquis had removed from my rucksack were in my car.

I should see about food. I still have a few tuna packets lying around somewhere and plenty of water.

The Elder Tablet is nestled wrapped in a towel from the bathroom. I left most of my gear in the car. Tomorrow, I'll get in touch with MJ. There's truly nothing left for me in New Jersey. The Marquis told me to seek them out after the ritual, but there is no way I can get back to Seaside Heights now. At the shelter, I heard about the ocean meeting the bay just north of where the monolith sat. What five, maybe six miles away? That was what ruptured the protections at the monolith. That was what tore the Jet-Star off its moorings. That was what ripped the Deep Ones City from beneath the waves. I am certain that's what those coral tiles were.

I'll have plenty to puzzle over when I get back to Sentinel Street. I'm sure I'll discover if my ritual was successful. As soon as I can return, I will seek out the Marquis. Perhaps he can lend some guidance in deciphering the Tablet. Both its intent and the reason it came to me.

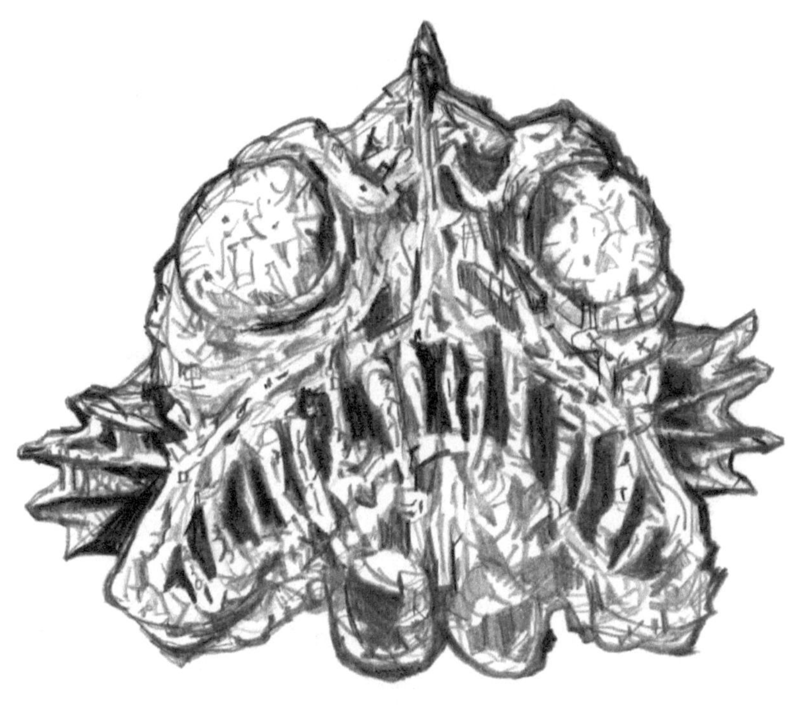

ACT IIII
2019

JEREMIAH

July 21ˢᵗ 2019 6:45pm

Didn't Charles Lamb warn us? Warn me? Didn't he once say: "Hydras and Chimaeras reproduce themselves in the brain of superstition—*but they were there before."* Didn't he acknowledge that "they are transcripts, archetypes in us. Eternal. How else is it that we naturally conceive terror from such objects? *These terrors are of older standing. They date beyond body—* That the kind of fear is purely spiritual—that it is a peep at least into the shadowland of pre-existence."

That is where I stand. I suppose I should have listened more closely, kept a more open mind. But, I was rash. I went too far too quickly and without the consideration of the intention. The realization. I am here, helter skelter beyond the borders of Lamb's Shadowlands.

I might be at the point now where I should have been when I first was given the Tablet, belched forth as it was by the All-Father himself, what was it, six years ago now? No. Come this Autumn, seven.

But, when the Tablet was first given to me, I was stronger, more able to conceive of the power held in this thing. Now?

I have been at a disarray and I am beginning anew. This is my first journal entry in over seventeen months. I was released from Arkham maybe month ago. Maybe two? My sense of time has certainly shifted. All that Haldol I suppose. I can sense it leaving my system, but it may take some time for my energies to come back, to come full. For me to activate again.

I won't waste time, space or energy to backtrack the last several months, but I have to say that I have royally fucked up. The Marquis was right. My last and gravest mistake was not to return to the temple on Carteret immediately after the ritual.

But how could I? Seaside Heights was under water for days. And with the repeated winter storms that followed Sandy? Much of the area was closed off to everyone for weeks. How could I have gotten back there? I do not have the benefit of his blasted flippers.

But the monolith was untouched. Perhaps the temple would be still there? In a protective bifurcation in space. A protective fold...why did I not try? Not even after the rebuilding, after the restoration?

I did not go back to Seaside Heights for what seemed like years. It wasn't. But...was I afraid? Perhaps. Perhaps I wanted the Tablet for myself.

No perhaps. I wanted the Tablet for myself. It was mine. It came to me. My own. My precious. Should I add a gollum after that? MJ wouldn't have it any other way.

MJ. I royally fucked matters there too. Still. Maybe not irreversible. She did get me back my car and my papers, my journal and of course the Elder Tablet. Though she didn't fully know what she was granting me access to. Just the undesignated pastiche of JEREMIAH'S THINGS.

She scrawled it on the boxes. Neatly packed, but in no order. Or at least no order I would have stipulated. I was pleased that two things occurred when MJ and I can presume Donna gathered up my materials. First, no one snooped. MJ visited me, once, but I was too drugged to really comprehend what she was babbling about. She didn't say anything about anything, really. Had she found my writings, my deciphering of the Tablet, or the Tablet itself, she would have said something. Or I would have been visited by the entire Armitage Division with their little bags and beady eyeballs.

Two, my wards held. Despite the shaving and the Haldol and the restraints. I kept my most important papers, my ritual tools in an old footlocker, locked of course. But warded also. The key is kept around my neck at all times— except when I was at Arkham of course. But the key was simply held with my wallet and et ceteras until my release. Had my wards been broken, I would have known someone had also been breaking into the locker.

Nothing of the kind happened. So that brings me here.

It would only serve to repeat myself if I were to trace backwards from now until then. There on the monolith. Cataloging all my mistakes. Not going back to the temple perhaps the start of a snowball of them because that led to my going back to school and my being compelled enough to try and secret away that last selection from A. Gordon Pym's Antartica journal. His notes were the first time I had encountered a phonetic account of the language. I managed to transcribe bits in my own documentation, but that was the final overstepping. They found the section I had removed from the folder. It wasn't even bound. Just a jumble of papers in a leather wrapping. I took too many pages. I'm sure that's how they knew that anything was missing. That, and I had requested it on quite a number of occasions. I mean it wasn't like I tried stealing the *Unaussprechlichen Kulten* or anything.

That wasn't my last mistake though. The snowball kept rolling on and on.

It was all because of the Tablet. Of course it was. How could it not be? Pym knew. He managed to crack some of it and that was what a century BEFORE the blasted Pabodie Expedition?   And we know how that one fared. And Pym was before the Erebus and the Terror and all that disaster in the ice up North. If it wasn't for Pym I wouldn't be able to read what I can.

Pym came face to face with Lamb's terrors though. He wrote of the Elder cities and their infernal breeding pits. So, he did overcome his spiritual fear. I mean, he cracked their language and he wrote it down. And, I know he had to have survived. How? I read his fucking journal. And because of Dr. Danforth.

Figures Danforth is involved. Fucking Nora Pym Danforth. Every time I turn around that woman is there. Why? What is the pattern *there*? She is my hydra, my chimaera, my bane.

Maybe I should include her in my current focus? My need to regain what has been taken from me...

I never did glean her connection to Pym. Unmarried harridan that she is, Pym Danforth isn't her husband's name. Who am I to question her association with names? I can hear MJ in my head. Hypocrite much, *Jeremiah Allen D'Bourget Curwen. You know, the only people to have four names are serial killers and encyclopedia salesmen.* Cue tittering laugher.

I'm being unfair. MJ has brought me back my purpose, though. In a sense. I'm here now, writing again because she saved my things from the local landfill.

But I think perhaps now, as I hunker down here, in the remains of Mrs. McGovern's old shack on Minturn— funny how life takes you back and back and back until you get things right? If I stay here, now that I have my documents again, now that I have my journal and my papers and my tools back again. It's good to be surrounded with my things.... Now that I have the Tablet again, I can learn anew or remember what the Haldol has tried to erase.

I have Pym's notes. What I kept. I think I might be able to access the photos I took on my phone, too. Of the material I didn't yet transcribe. There's no point in reactivating any account, but I believe after a nice charge, I should be able to access the images.

I can't be bothered by logging though. There will be no posterity in paper. Not for me. I suppose I wanted to have another entry to end my journal, perhaps. My last one can't be the sob-story about MJ kicking me out of Sentinel Street, about my getting the final boot from university— the only student to ever be officially barred from the Orne and finally expelled from school. Well since old Wally Gilman that is. It's a rare honor, but not one I care to delve too deeply. Suffice it to say, despite my attempts to get back in the school's good graces— even if merely to make use of its vast resources— I could not. The Tablet occupied me.

I also found myself without my guides, since I have also fell out of favor with the Marquis. After that night on the monolith, I no longer see the sigils. I have no guides to push me this way or that. Nothing to tell me what to read or how to learn this infernal language with any credence.

Other than what I gleaned from Pym. But Pym I don't believe, had a complete understanding.

Oh I can read the Tablet. Make no mistake. But, mentally. To myself. Aloud? The inflections are so nuanced that a difference in a syllable can be the difference between calling up a servant or a master, a daemon of the pit or marshmallow fluff.

I have to try. I was put on this path. The All-Father gave me the Tablet. Told me to use it. Either the creature will bring me to completion, like Curwen, to become the All-in-One, the me-yet-to-be, a creature of limitless being. Or, it will lay waste to mine enemies. There's always the chance that the extra bit, the few lines I haven't quite teased out might be the final bit to call forth Father Dagon.

The Marquis, I imagine, never got this far. Despite his being over a dozen times my age.

How dare he abandon me though? I am his blood. His kin. The last of his line, perhaps? How could he dangle such wonders before me only to have such an unreasonable expectation that I would be able to override the authorities of our own military to run back to a devastation zone? To what? Say hi?

The Marquis must learn that he was the one who erred. Not I. He along with those damnable Allens.

Donna was the one who signed the order after all, granting permission for me Jeremiah D'Bourget Curwen to be committed. She had no right. The day she did that, I resolved to remove her name from my own. Well, her husband's name.... I am no longer an Allen. Nor shall I use the D'Bourget name either. Removing both should remove the associations. I will be beholden to neither the Allens nor the Marquis.

I shall simply be Jeremiah Curwen. Yog-Sothoth take them all. The Allens. The Marquis. Pym fucking Danforth and the Armitage division. Jaimie with his meathead and stupid brogue wearing one of those damnable kilts no less like he was Dagon's gift. I'll have a special creature set aside for him, *Outlander* wanna-be.

I should be successful this time. The last effort did naught to teach them a lesson. Naught to wipe them from existence, as the Marquis *instructed me to do!*

He lied, as did Donna, Marvin, even MJ! How could she? Standing there telling me that she and Jaimie no longer needed my— what did she call it— bad mojo hanging around the house?

She could barely speak to me without Jaimie standing there. For moral support. And who's all about women standing up for themselves? She needed a man to tell me to hit the road.

Lucky the fucker wasn't in his kilt. I would have strangled him with it.

And don't get me started about being denied by the All-Mother Herself. Had I not been rejected, tossed out of the crack in space-time atop the monolith, I would have been in a position to go back to the Marquis. Instead of being scooped up by harbor patrol. That was Her doing.

Well. I shall show them all, won't I?

I hear the calling in my mind. In my dreams. I am the me-yet-to-be, the one from all those moons ago, dreaming on the shores of Crystal Lake.

They did shave most of my hair though, just after I was first admitted. But, after I started "to comply" it was a reward to allow me to start growing it back. After the first two months. I even became a bit of a joke with the orderlies and Alton, the only one who was actually nice to me. I mean he didn't take my chocolate pudding away that time he found I had been hoarding it. But that's a different story. He actually showed me how to get my hair to come back. He showed me how to backcomb it, thinking it was funny that a skinny little mo'fo like me wanted dreads. Once, he showed me a picture of himself, from nursing school with a set that would have made Bob Marley jealous. Alton wasn't permitted dreadlocks when he became an Arkham member of staff. Too easy for patients to get a handhold.

But, they became my power. Not unlike Sampson I suppose.

Before my stint in Arkham, I had already found my tattoo. The tall one from the Union Café, the one who painted the grand mural of the Magna Mater gave me the first. Though she wouldn't even consider a large piece without my first giving her a deposit. MJ thought I was insane, that first tattoo. Especially seeing how I'm allergic to squid.

Now whenever anyone sees it, like Alton and the nurses, they figure I'm a *Game of Thrones* fan. I always suspected good ol' George RR was one of them. He has a bit of the Innsmouth look. Fucking poser, between his Drowned God and the squid motto? What is dead may never die. Indeed.

He's lucky the All-Father doesn't drown him. But I'm meandering again.

I'm out. I should be grateful. There is a sliver of humanity left which reprimands me, silences the howl, the rage, and tells me to be grateful.

MJ and Donna did pay for storage. Why I couldn't tell you. I was thoroughly terrified of MJ's precious Nora Danforth getting her disgusting paws on the Elder Tablet. I knew she would reclaim it for the university. After all, it had been part of their Special Collections.

However, it was liberated more than once and at some point it must have been returned to its proper place. Danforth always took an interest in the Tablet. She said it was her father's find. Her father being the same Danforth who taught Psychology at Miskatonic for all those years. After he recovered from his own mental breakdown while on that expedition with Professor Dyer.

I mean, with all her background, all her learning, all her expanded magnanimous bullshit, you'd think Dr. Nora Jean Pym Danforth would understand about a mental fucking break. Her father was batshit after what he saw in 1928.

But I'm doing exactly what Alton told me I do. Jump from one thing to another and never get to the fucking point.

Thanksgiving. Grace. Appreciation.

Donna had me committed, but she also held my things. MJ had already kicked me out. I had no place to go. Donna was between Warren, Rhode Island, and Toms River. She happened to be heading back to New Jersey, with misfit Marvin of course, right when MJ said I had one of my final-straw fits. She and Jaimie closed their door to me and I was left in the rain. I really don't recall what happened next. Just that I woke up in the passenger seat and Donna was driving my car back to New Jersey. We had just crossed the Outerbridge and I suppose most of the trip she had some peace since I was out cold. All my worldly possessions once again filling what Marvin called the two-body trunk and the backseat of my retired police cruiser. Marvin followed along behind, I suppose.

That itself had been a lucky find all those years ago. The summer before Miskatonic. I still have the thing. My car I mean. Rescued as it was from the jaws of the Magna Mater. It was rescued again and again. After getting back to Jersey, Donna found me a room to rent next door to where her old friend, the Minturn Witch had disappeared. Donna and Marvin had finally sold the house on Buchanan and were moving with permanence to Rhode Island.

I stayed here for a time. I suppose that's why I came back. The house is empty. Has been since the McGoverns left. After their aunt, or whoever the old witch was to them, disappeared, the younger McGoverns took possession of the property. Yeah, nephew. The guy was her nephew. Inherited her house and her Halloween collection. After Sandy, he snapped up the property next door and rented me one of the rooms. He had a mind to make a killing during beach season or something. Though none of his other boarders stayed long. Said I gave them the creeps.

But then I made the mistake of going back to Arkham. Back to face MJ and Danforth and demand access to the library again.

How else was I to finish my work?

Of course there was a moment when I tried to recite the incantations from memory, but that was when I was hospitalized.

Donna wasn't even there when she granted permission to commit. She did it over the phone.

Gratitude is nice, but it also means beholden. And even though they both stored my things, my car too, at that storage place only a few blocks away, back on Route 37— I shall not be beholden to anyone. Maybe Donna felt guilty? After she granted permission? After they shaved my head I suppose. The McGoverns moved and told Donna they would be selling both properties— that unless my stuff was taken by my family, it would be thrown away.

So Donna packed everything into storage while MJ and fucknut Jaime drove my car down from Arkham. MJ told me when I was in my stupor at Arkham.

As soon as I am of my old strength, I shall take yet another peep into the Shadowland of pre-existence again. Then we'll see how what I can say might be my final hand is played out.

HEKLA
ICELAND
63°58'58.8"N, 19°39'57.6"W; SUMMIT ELEV. 1490 M

Elevated seismicity during July-August 2019

On 15 August 2019, the Icelandic Meteorological Office (IMO) began detecting micro-earthquakes at Hekla. The IMO detected at least 7 high-frequency earthquakes whose magnitudes ranged from 0.4-1. The earthquakes were recorded over a small area approximately 4.5 km to the NE of Hekla's summit with a source 11-12 km below the surface. The earthquakes were judged as the result of brittle fracture rather than a consequence of magma moving. It is important to note a clustering of earthquakes such as these is uncommon during non-eruption periods at Hekla.

On 18 August 2019, the IMO began detecting an earthquake swarm off the coast of Reykjanes peninsula on Reykjanes ridge. At least 1742 high-frequency earthquakes whose magnitudes ranged from 0.4-2.2. The earthquake swarm is located 2-4 km south-west of Geirfugladrangur Rock over a small area approximately with a source 10-32 km below the surface. The earthquakes may note the consequence of magma moving. It is unclear if this earthquake swarm is over.

93

BSA TROOP 38: BOYD ELEMENTARY SCHOOL

"Ok, Charlie, EJ, Lily, and Mia, you're not at the camporee any more. If you don't stop with the friggin' bottle bashing, we're going to say bye-bye to finishing this weather station, ok? You've already crunched two bottles and this is why they don't want us back at the church. You guys got out of hand."

"Yes, Troop Leader," apologized a chorus of voices, one boy and the rest girls. They were meeting in the back of Troop Leader Brady's science class, despite the fact that all the scouts in his troop attended intermediate school on the mainland. It was just easier since the kids lived here and he taught here. Besides, after the whole brouhaha with the Roman Catholic Church on the mainland, Troop Leader Brady figured it wasn't worth the hassle. Besides, he might be able to get a few of his sixth graders interested in removing their brains from the technological void of television, social media, and gaming to maybe learn some stuff the old fashioned way.

"Now, we've got everything in place, but the rain gauge. I want to build four of them. So, one each. Just incase something gets messed up this week, we know we've got a backup. Also, we'll be able to do some experiments on the side, test things like acidity and stuff like that. And, if we keep all four up and running, we can try different durations on each. Like a day, week, month, or something plus a control. You decide that. We have the weather merit badge worksheet and it would be neat to see if we can measure some environmental impacts for each element of our weather station. We've got to consider each element— from temperature to air speed to rainfall, both amount and content as in pollution, you know. And see what the possible impacts are. Ok. Now you're on point, guys. I'm done talking. Who's doing the demo again?"

The tallest of the troop, raises his hand.

"Ok, Charlie, you're up then."

The boy takes several moments to explain and then demonstrate the creation of a rain gauge using a clear soda bottle, a ruler, and some tape. "Now here's my own devising." He said with a sparkle, rubbing his hands together melodramatically and then producing a block of purple stuff from beneath the small desk he had been working at. "Modeling clay. It's the key to getting the bottom of the bottle even and is way better than some other stuff you see online like sand, rocks, even Jell-O."

"What about dish soap? I saw that too," asked EJ, the most recent addition to Troop 38.

"Could contaminate the samples and we can't then test for acidity. Soap's a base, so when we do the other tests, it might neutralize anything else. So, get the clay and shove it in like this. You gotta work it in there. I'm using a small, flat bottom jar to get the top of the clay smooth, as flat as possible, while getting the underneath into all the bumps in the bottom of the jar. Then put in your ruler, and finish the assembly. But, before you put in the funnel, you know the inverted top of the bottle, we're going to add a few drops of oil."

"Won't that contaminate the sample?"

"It shouldn't. I don't think so, but—"

"Why do we need to add the oil then? Why risk contamination?"

"EJ, let Charlie finish his response to your question."

"Sorry, Troop Leader Brady."

"Thanks. Yeah, the weather's been so hot that by the time we check the levels, especially if we get say a few hot days in between rainfall, whatever's collected already will just evaporate. Remember we're trying 3 different measurement techniques to see how much rain falls in a day, a week, a month—so we want to see if there's any contradictions in the amounts. Stuff like that."

"Ok, Troop, let's finish up our rain gauges and get them with the station. We're marking each one so we know which has which duration. Make corresponding notes on your weather logbooks. And I want you to keep your data by hand."

This was met with an assortment of groans.

"That shouldn't surprise you. We're also going to try something else— keeping the weather station in different locations. This is a longterm side project, ok? Charlie, you'll get the station first."

"I object to the implicit misogyny in the system," Lily blurted out.

"Huh?"

"Troop Leader Brady, why does he get it first? I object to the implicit misogyny inherent in the system."

"Yeah!" Lily's sister Mia echoed "He's just getting it first because he's your son. That's nepotism, Troop Leader Brady. I'm telling my dad."

"You do that hon. You forget who got to orchestrate last year's haunted house? You and your sister. This is the project we're doing right now. Charlie was the one who brought it to the Troop. You two were in charge of last year's project. So, let's come up with the next one as a group. Any thoughts?"

"Start an animal rescue?"

"Knit hats for frogs."

"Adopt a homeless family of ferrets."

"Let's focus on this one and come up with some more ideas. Yeah-huh?"

AUGUST 20TH 2019
SWELTERING HEAT CONTINUES

"Those hazy, hot, and humid August days aren't going anywhere anytime soon. I'm Liz Cho, Bill will be with you at the 11 o'clock and Mayor DeBlasio has declared a state of emergency because of the heat, has called in extra Con Ed workers to handle any outages, and has advised office buildings to turn the thermostat up to 78° to conserve energy. Meanwhile, across the Hudson, in Newark it was a really dangerous day to be outside in this heat. One place where folks don't mind the soaring temperatures is the beach. Here's a live look at Seaside Heights where you can see lots of people still there; it's 6 o'clock in the evening.

"We have several reports tonight. We have Toni Yates in Seaside Heights and Tim Fleischer is in the East Village, but we are going to begin with our meteorologist Lee Goldberg. He's outside our studios on the upper west side. Lee."

"Liz. It's pretty easy to just wilt in this hot wind. This shirt has no chance of seeing the 11 o'clock . You just sweat right through.

This hot wind is just a blowtorch breeze. All right, now not only do we have the hot weather, we have some thunderstorms for Mount Holly, Brick, and Toms River with heavy downpours, gusting winds, lightning. We might even have a tornado watch for parts of Burlington and Ocean counties. We're watching a circular pattern moving over the area.

"We have an excessive heat warning for the entire Tristate area for the next couple of days. There's an advisory for upper Ulster County. Air quality alert will be poor through until the weekend. There it is. We waited until 6:00 and still we get 90°. Just about the lowest temperature we've seen since nearly midnight, when we clocked in at 89°. The heat wave is now official. We hovered around 89 for a couple of hours early morning, then went strait back to the 90s by the morning commute. Right now, it feels like 100°.

"So 90 in the Park. 92 Belmar. 94 in Toms River. The only places that are comfortable are Islip, Montauk, and Bridgeport because of the water off of the Sound and off the ocean. The feel like reading: up to 110 in Morristown and Toms River. I mean that's after starting out with clouds today and having to dry out all the rains from the last couple of days? With the remnants of Howard. It's not even a tropical depression any longer, but still it's bringing in that line of rough weather across parts of the Mid-Atlantic. So this is really impressive heat. Look at the line of lightening and thunderstorms moving across central Pennsylvania, drifting into Mercer, Middle-sex, Monmouth, Ocean, Burlington, maybe even down into Camden. So a few of those will be with us for the next couple of hours, but they'll just fizzle away and we'll be left with a warm, stuffy night.

"We're hovering around 90 for several hours here and it will feel like 90 until about midnight here in New York City. So fierce heat for the next few days. Take it seriously! Really brace yourself. You know a lot of times you say, you know it's summer and it's hot. But this is a different type of heat. We haven't experienced this in a while. It will be near 100 on the thermometer. It will feel like 110 to 115. We'll have some spotty storms, but we'll have to wait for some relief maybe later in the week, or early next week. Much more on that in the 7-day forecast in just a little bit. Liz, back to you for now."

CALLER: "Hello? Hello?"

DISPATCH: "911. Where's your emergency?"

CALLER: (Inaudible. Breathing heavily.) "Toms River police. There's screaming. I don't know if there was a shot. There was a loud noise like someone shooting. But, then somebody was trying to break into my house and attack my mom. Fucking dog was barking and then—" (Inaudible.)

DISPATCH: "Ok, sir. Where are they shooting at? Where are you located?"

CALLER: (Breathing heavily) "Just send the police. Toms River."

DISPATCH: "Ok, sir. I'm going to need you to calm down and tell me your location. Where are you at?"

CALLER: "89 Bay Shore Drive." (Inaudible)

DISPATCH: "There were gunshots fired? And somebody's trying to get into the house?

CALLER: "I don't know. There was a loud bang and something happened. Like maybe an explosion. Lightning. Fucking boom. Dunno." (Inaudible) " It was weird. Maybe he had an M80." (Inaudible; voices on the caller's side. Garbled.)

DISPATCH: (talking to someone else) "Reported shots fired on Bay Shore Drive, Toms River."

DISPATCH: "And was he the only shooter?"

CALLER: "I told you I don't know if he was shooting. But, he was screaming and there was this loud crash or a bang. I told you. The fucking sky lit up. But," (Inaudible.) "He was, yeah by himself. He came after her with some stick and this weird stone thing. Like Moses."

DISPATCH: "Excuse me? What was that?"

CALLER: "Dude had something in his hand." (Breathing heavily; shouting in the background)

DISPATCH: "A weapon?"

CALLER: "Don't know what it was. He was waving his arms around. Shouting. Yelling at our house. Then the explosions started. Or gunshots. Whatever they were."

CALLER: "Where are you? Inside the house?"

CALLER: "Yes. Now we are. But when it started? We were in the yard with the barbecue. He just came up to her and started freaking out. Dog started going nuts. All of them did."

DISPATCH: "All of who, sir? Your family?"

CALLER: "No." (Inaudible) "Fucking dogs. Every one of them in the neighborhood started yapping their heads off. And my neighbor's dog got pulled into the canal like by a fucking alligator or something." (Inaudible; shouting on the caller's side) "No!" (Breathing heavily) "Send someone, would you? We need help."

DISPATCH: "Units have been dispatched, sir. Stay on the line. Do you know who he is?"

CALLER: "No. He's some guy.

DISPATCH: "Can you describe him?"

CALLER: "Some young guy, ma'am. He's wearing a grey robe and what looks like boxer shorts. Sorry, shit's getting real here. Something's going on now—"

DISPATCH: "What's happening now?"

CALLER: "He's out there now. Went back to standing in the street. Shouting." (Other voices on caller's side inaudible.) "I can let you hear him. He's standing in the middle of the fucking street screaming his head off like something from the *Exorcist* ma'am."

DISPATCH: "Calm down, sir. Are you safe?"

CALLER: "I don't know about safe." (Breathing heavily). "He's still out there, I said. I think I just heard another shot."

DISPATCH: "Can you see the shooter? Did you see a gun?"

CALLER: "No. I'm not going out to look though. The patio behind me is open. We're on the fucking floor, here. You can hear him if I hold the phone up. He's coming down into yard again, heading toward the water. Listen:

"Y'AI'NG'NGAH YOG-SOTHOTH H'EE-L'GEB F'AI THRODOG UAAAH Y'AI'NG'NGAH SHOG-GOTH FK'EE-FK'GLEB HA'F'AI THRODOG IA! IAAAAAA....."

CALLER: "Fucker's in my back yard. He's waving that thing over his head. What the fuck is that thing—" (Garbled.)

"TEKELI-LITEKELI-LITEKELI-LIIIIIIIIIII....."

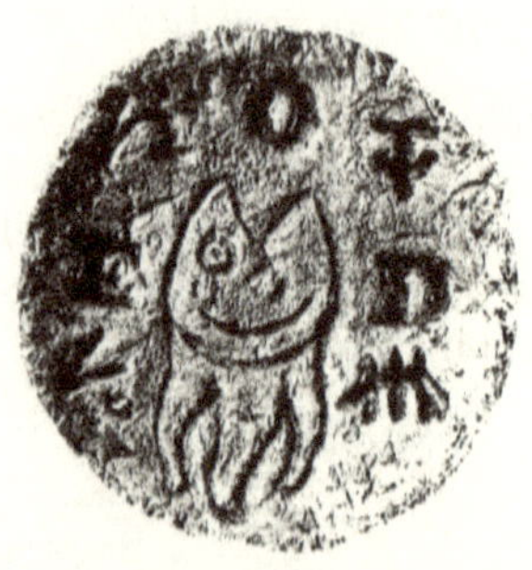

BREAKING NEWS:
THE GATEWAY TO HELL MAY BE OPENING

"I'm Bill Ritter everyone and tonight at 11, we have some unusual news to report. Yes, you heard that right. What's called the 'Gateway to Hell' may be opening, in addition to the sweltering grip this heat has on the city. We have this just in from, Iceland. Yes, Iceland. We have another volcano, Hekla often called the 'Gateway to Hell', which has started raging. Fears are that this one might just send another dust cloud our way. Already flights in the area are being cancelled and we have some air traffic being grounded. But, even before we get into that, Ladies and Gentlemen, um— Sade?"

"Yes, Bill. Sorry, but I was getting an update there. We seem to have something happening down at the Jersey Shore. Reports of a possible shooting off the Thomas A. Mathis Bridge toward Seaside Heights. This is breaking news and we'll report it as we get more information, but for right now, I'm being told that we may have a hostage situation. Possibly, let me get this right, an alligator sighting? We're sending someone to the scene and will get you that information just as soon as we do. We'll head over to Lee at the weather-desk in a moment. But, Bill, about that volcano?"

"Alligators? Riiiight...Sade. Sources at the Icelandic Meteorological Office are saying that Mount Hekla, one of Iceland's most active volcanoes, started waking up this morning with a massive, um, what's called an 'earthquake swarm?' A few miles off off the Ricky-jane peninsula—"

"That's more of a y sound Bill, the Reykjanes peninsula."

"Thanks Sade. The Ricky-jane peninsula had over a thousand small level earthquakes and experts fear that may have started things off. Hekla is about 100 miles from the capital of Ricky-yavik, but Hekla isn't called the Mouth of Hell for nothing."

"Yeah, Bill. Reykjavik. Hekla is one of Iceland's largest volcanoes and has often woken up with little or no warning. Sometimes seismic activity starting only 30 minutes before an eruption, Bill. Hekla's history dates back to over a thousand years, with the first major earthquake on record in 1104. Hold on, Bill, let me get this right. Remember back in 2010 when EY-ya-FYA-htla-YUH-kuhtl stalled air traffic? There was only almost 100,000 flights cancelled over a travel ban that lasted little more than a week. Half of the world's air traffic ground to a standstill because of the plume of ash and debris belched forth by that volcano."

"Belched forth, I like that Sade. Yes, well I've got to try it as well E-ya-FayA-hatlA-Yokel-coatl— sounds like that Aztec God? I don't think I got that right, but that one erupted for 96 days and it caused such devastation—"

"From the lava?"

"From my understanding, no. From the ash cloud. This one? Hekla? It can erupt for *years.* One eruption started in 1845 and lasted for almost 2 *years.*"

"How is that possible, Bill?"

"I don't know. Ask Lee. It's science. But, Hekla has another funny feature, besides the lava and the ash. Because of the mineral content of its 'tephra' –you know all the bits that get vomited up into the air? How'd you like that, vomited. You said belched— so I've got to one-up-you, there. Ha. With Hekla, the tephra is rich in fluorine that can kill livestock. So, get your cattle inside, Icelandic farming persons and anyone in need of a mountainous hike, beware of 'incandescent pyroclastic flows' ontop of the lava and the ash cloud. What, do they glow or something?"

"I think they're the same thing, Bill. The wall of ash, gas, and debris is the pyroclastic flow. That right Lee? And how are we doing with this heat? Will any of this gloom and doom stuff affect the weather? Any rain of toads in the seven-day?"

C6776: "Charlie 6-7-7-6. Central."

DISPATCH: "C6776 Go ahead."

C6776: "Victim DOA with obvious head trauma. Witnesses confused. Some said suspect fled across the Tunney Bridge, on 37. Others said the blob ate him and jumped in the canal off Bay Shore Drive. We've also got a report of an alligator sighting. Fucking shit down here. Send available units for containment. I repeat, send all available units."

DISPATCH:"Repeat that C6776. EMS notified and en route. Do they need to stage or is it safe to approach?"

C6776: "EMS? No pulse on subject." (inaudible) "Guy's head is gone. Send available units."

COMMUNITY MEDICAL CENTER, RT 37 TOMS RIVER

CHARGE NURSE: "What'd you bring me? A live one? I love them. And a midnight burrito too. Love me a live midnight burrito even more."

EMT: "We saved this one special for you. Some shit's going down at the shore, so units will be following. This here is Jeremiah. No ID. He's a screamer. Don't know what he's on about though. Can't understand a word of it."

CHARGE NURSE: (over unintelligible screams) "How'd you get him? 911? What is that? Sounds like a dolphin." (to another nurse) "Get security in here. All hands."

EMT: "PD. Toms River resident reported gunshots, one DOA on the scene, and this guy menacing his mother."

CHARGE NURSE: "This guy's mother?" (directing another nurse) "Give me a Haldol night-cap. 5:1."

EMT: "Caller's mother. Said Jeremiah was in his jammies here was shouting in the street and they took cover when they heard a shot. Something about an animal attack too. Not my deal. PD picked this guy up wandering on foot across the Route 37 Bridge. Tossed his bathrobe at a motorist. Only thing he said that made any sense when we zipped him up here, was: 'Jeremiah must find the Maquis.' Maybe he's a Star Trek fan?"

CHARGE NURSE: "Huh?"

EMT: "*Voyager?* Chakotay's original crew?"

CHARGE NURSE: "Riiight. We got a four-point here and you're talking geek? How you know he's Jeremiah?"

EMT: "Don't. No ID. Figured he looked all Biblical and shit. Jeremiah suits him. PD should be right behind us."

CHARGE NURSE: "Under arrest? He cuffed?"

EMT: "Yeah. Might be. Like I said, PD got a DOA over on Bay Shore, near where we picked up this guy. They've got their hands full on Barrier Island. But, yeah— Here they are."

OFFICER: (Breathing heavily) "Here we have Johnny Doe. No identification."

EMT: "We've been calling him Jeremiah. He seems to like that name, don't you Jeremiah?"

CHARGE NURSE: "Like the bullfrog? Better than John Doe."

OFFICER: "Might just be the neighborhood rummy, but we subdued him on Tunney Bridge. He's clearly drunk and disorderly. But, he's also a person of interest in a homicide. But that could be an animal attack. Some benny might've let a gator loose for s-and-gs."

CHARGE NURSE: "Right, then. Jeremiah, hon, you ready for your close-up? Let's unwrap him my darlings."

"Breakin' news, yo! This is Funguy from the Jersey Shore. We came in from New Dorp dis mornin' lookin' to rock out the summer here in da' Heights and we iz here on Boulevard lookin' for action. But lookie here. What is that fucker man? What are we lookin' at Big Larry D?"

"Yo Funguy, bro. I got this dog. Fucker's messed up, man. Ain't this some shit. Go poke that thing with a stick!"

"What's that the broomstick ya had up yo ass? That ain't no dog, Larry D. Is it a gator? Nah Yo! Hit it again man! Looks like my ma's calamari. Fucker ate that dog. You saw it. Took it right under that fuckin' car."

"Dude, you see that? What the fuck are those things, and that sound? Them fuckin' eyes? You shittin' me. This is some sick movie prop shit."

"TEKELI-LITEKELI-LITEKELI-TEKELI-LITEKKELLLIIIIIIII....."

DR. HALSEY

This is Dr. Gilbert Halsey, Attending Physician at Toms River Psychiatric Unit. Here are my case notes, transcribed from my audio notes, patient statement, and audio recording of my first and only session, for the morning of Wednesday, August 21st, 2019. 1130 hrs.

This is my personal account of the situation as given in evidence to the Armitage Research Division on September 1st, 2019.

The patient was transferred to us early this morning, shortly after he was taken into custody. Things got crowded at the ED and he was quickly transported under sedation. Patient has no identification. Fingerprints revealed that he is officially identified as Jeremiah Allen D'Bourget of Arkham, Massachusetts. He is a caucasian male, approximately 26 years of age, Height 5'11, and undernourished at 145 pounds.

Jeremiah was not placed under arrest, however he has been detained for mandatory observation while the police investigate his possible connection to the murder of a man, name yet to be released. Jeremiah was assumed drunk, but his blood had no alcohol levels. He presented as delusional and rather agitated.

After sedation, Nurse Grace Theremin drew blood for varied panels and further toxicology since initial screening did not test beyond the basics. Something bizarre is going on and I ordered a few more tests. Jeremiah came into Community late last night. He slept for just under 5 hours before he began shouting. The things he says are more than bizarre. He was given a booster of Haldol, which did calm him down. Jeremiah was conscious and panicked as I addressed him.

My first audio session is as follows with my observations interjected. Again, this was the only session with Mr. Allen. Nurse Theremin left with the blood-work. The door was closed for privacy.

"Hello Mr. Allen, are you ready to talk with me? I'm Dr. Halsey. I hope you're feeling calmer. The medication we gave you should help. I do hope you're feeling better. The restraints are for your safety and that of my staff."

"W— wha? Where am I?"

"It's ok, just take a deep breath and relax for me. Mr. Allen, can I ask you a few questions...?"

"Jeremiah. Call me Jeremiah. I'm not a fucking Allen."

"Ok, Jeremiah. Can we talk about what brought you here?"

Jeremiah seemed to go rigid. I noted that we might need an EEG since he presented as having somewhat of a seizure disorder. I must note if these are Haldol induced seizures and review his medications. Without an EEG, there's no telling the type, so for now: unknown onset seizure with focal awareness. He presented as having tonic-myoclonic-atonic seizures in a repeated pattern for the first 65 seconds. Rigidity of upper extremities. Neck tendons visible. The restraints on his wrists kept him from leaping off the bed. Tonic episode lasted approximately 21 seconds, followed by a myoclonic episode of about 17 seconds. Jerking became rather violent. I rang for assistance and the spell ended with an atonic episode of 27 seconds whereupon he fell back against the pillows seemingly insensate. This cycle repeated for the next 2.5 minutes.

The nurse came in as the patient regained some gross motor function. He began to scream in a tongue I had not heard before, a gurgling, croaking multi-syllabic phrase, repeating it three times. Nurse Theramin was prepared with Keppra, but without the proper scans, I can't presume to start such a treatment. Though if the seizures continue, that will be on the table.

As he thrashed, not at risk of immediate injury, I scanned him. Hair, an unkept mass of stringy brown coils. Face hidden in a derangement of beard. His hands had the look of someone on the street for some time. Xerosis cutis on the hands and lower arms. Seemingly from excessive scrubbing since the skin is manifestly raw, cracked in places, particularly on the knuckles and between the fingers. Yet his face and lower extremities look as though he hasn't bathed in days. He had been placed in the standard patient "pajamas". During his episode, his shirt rose up, revealing the outline of more coils, black, imprinted on his flesh. I could see from the neckline were more black squiggles interspersed with strange scarring. As he thrashed his head, I could see a further evidence of xerosis cutis, possibly psoriasis alongside what appeared to be three jagged diagonal lines recently cut into his neck. This was not observable earlier because of his hair and beard.

"Interesting. Are those tattoos Jeremiah, may I look?"

Nodding heavily, he seemed to have a momentary Postictal dysphasia and was unable to speak. There don't seem to be other post-seizure behaviors. No paralysis or automatisms, although he kept wriggling his nose. Perhaps, had he not been in restraints, he might have been nose scratching. Possibly the sign of a complex partial seizure.

I proceeded to lift his shirt the rest of the way. On his chest was a large Humboldt squid, tentacles pointed up, brushing his collarbone. I looked at his arms and saw small strange fish like faces clustered upon his upper right arm. The patient sat forward, causing me to jump back thinking he was about to bite or head butt me. I did not take notice earlier, due to his outburst following his episode, but now that he was calmer I noticed that yes, it might be a psoriasis around what appeared to be recently added scarification. But they didn't seem cut, rather burned into the flesh.

Already I saw signs of recovery from the postictal phase, as he began to speak without much stuttering.

"I'm ssttarting the change, doc. Kk. It's ok. The M-marquis didn't think I'd go this far. But, but. I'm O-K. Curious, doc?" He eyeballed his back. Smiled. "Lift my shirt and look at my back. I've got the ticket there. My invitation."

"The change, Jeremiah?"

"Can't fib. Not yet. See my back? Look."

Coming out of the post-seizure, he squirmed to the side, still in restraints. but I was able to inspect at his back from the top of his shirt, which hung rather loosely on him. I must tell Nurse Theremin to find him a smaller shirt. This one is far too large for him. Peering down, from the neckline, I saw a variety of interconnected tattoos, one of which looked like a fish staring up at me. It wasn't until later, after this session when he wasn't in the awkwardness of restraints that I was able to scrutinize the design more closely. It was a sign I was semi-familiar with: a fish-head, pointed upward with attached tentacles stretching downward. The letters EOD and curious runes had been inked around it.

Jeremiah's pupils contracted, his eyes narrowed, then widened again, protracting up at me with an intensity that as he sat back, I was concerned he would begin another episode. "Doc, you have to help me, I did something I should never have done and now it's too late."

I returned to my chair, asking, while noting the tattoos in my log, being sure to keep one eye on him for signs of a seizure. "What is it that you think you have done, Jeremiah?"

Sighing heavily, "It's not what I think I have done, Doc, but what I know I did. Doc? I can't call you Doc, like Bugs Bunny. What's your name again?"

"Dr. Halsey."

"Ok. Dr. Halsey. I fucked up. If I tell you to call someone, from Miskatonic University, you won't think I'm nuts? You'll help me?"

"Well, Jeremiah. You have been remanded to the custody of the Toms River Psychiatric Unit. Our job is to determine if you are, as you say, 'nuts.' Though let's not use that term, shall we? You seem to have had another emotional episode. Though, without more detail, I can't say if this is in any way similar to what you experienced in Massachusetts, for which you—" I consulted my notes. "Spent some time in the Arkham Sanitarium, is that correct?"

"Yes, but I'm not crazy. Well, maybe. But crazy people can

still make sense. I need you to call a friend of mine at Miskatonic. Madisen Berkana. She's the assistant to Dr. Nora Danforth in the Armitage Division."

Of course it had to be Nora Jean. I hadn't heard her name in years and hearing it for the first time was a bit of a shock. More than seeing a possible sign of the Order on a patient's back. Sorry, Nora since I know you'll be reading this. I know. I shouldn't have been that surprised. More than a few of Miskatonic's students found themselves at Arkham and if this one has been doing anything, shall we say, unusual for a lackluster term, then it would make sense for the Director of the spook-squad to be the one to call. Sorry, Nora. You know that was what we called your team. Anyway.

Jeremiah continued, alternating between a narrow, internal review of some memory, some deed, and an expanding expression as though he kept having to remind himself that he wasn't alone, but in a hospital. Again.

"Remember back during Sandy? That I think was partly my fault. What I did then amplified the storm. Made it much worse. I mean, a Cat 1 hurricane doing that much damage?"

"So you're telling me you were the cause of the destruction from Superstorm Sandy?" So delusions of grandeur. Noted.

"No. But, amplified? I'm a magician, Dr. Halsey."

"Like David Copperfield?"

"No, like Joseph Curwen, my ancestor. I was a student of the Occult, pursuing my degree at Miskatonic. You've got to call Dr. Danforth. To come out and investigate. Seven years ago during Superstorm Sandy, I found this Tablet on the beach—"

"Tablet? You mean like someone's i-pad?"

"No. A fucking stone tablet from what I can only imagine was an offshoot of Y'ha-nthlei. Although, that's back up the coast several hundred miles. I am certain, despite everything, *it's* still there. But, whatever might have been here— a suburb, a village, whateverthefuck. It's gone. Or damaged. Or was. But—whatever. I rode out the storm out by the Jet-Star. I was picked up by the coast guard. I was following instructions. I didn't go back to the Marquis, but I tried to. Just the other day. I went back to Hiering Street and I couldn't get back inside. I tried, but I fucked up I said."

"Inside? Inside what, Jeremiah?"

He answered in another torrent of words, barely taking a breath:

"The crack in space-time. Where I rode out the storm. Look, I told you. I was given the Tablet by the All-Father. I was directed to the monolith by the Marquis and the fish sigils, so I suppose by the Order too. He told me, the Marquis did, he told me what to do and I was supposed to set some cosmic chaos on my foster family, but instead I destroyed the Jersey shore. I was too strong. And then I was given the Tablet. Before I used the Tablet, last night I think. I mean, I don't know the day.... But, before I did use it, I went back like the Marquis told me to. I was late. I know. Seven years. Shit. But, at least I went back. When I did, I couldn't get in. The gateway was closed. And then I used the Tablet the first place I could. And then It came. Not the All-Father. No. Not even the Magna Mater. No. It came. I followed the instructions but...Don't fucking know what It was. But. It started eating...What have I done. They were HIS instructions? HE told me to do this? I shouldn't have...This shouldn't be happening. This shouldn't be happening. This—"

Jeremiah started rocking and repeating himself in a loop. He seemed to have thoroughly ceased any sunken, physically depressed, postictal calm, and seemed to be ramping up again. Though for another emotional or physical outburst, I couldn't say. I had to observe. I was cognizant that he could be experiencing some altered state of awareness due to an underlying seizure disorder. But, from his tattoos, I gathered he knew of the Esoteric Order of Dagon. I had to entertain some uncomfortable possibilities. Perhaps he was even a member in the area... those scars after all? Obviously a fledgling occultist, but also obviously held in the grip of some altered sensation. Although, I wonder. He's talking about something else, beneath the delusion, beneath any aural phase brought on by any neurological disorder. More sinister, if that can be believed. Although the brain can do some funny things....

"Where is this tablet now Jeremiah? What instructions are you speaking of? He who?" As I finished my questions, Jeremiah's body language went from the post-seizure relaxation I often privately called the noodle-state, to an almost maniacal state. He seemed to gear up for yet another seizure, body tightening, straining against the leather cuffs, his neck and head full of pulsating veins. This time, the scars on his now bulging throat opened. Gills? Not scars after all. Jeremiah's head snapped his head toward to me with an insect-like speed that caused a momentary panic.

He screamed. His *gills* now fully open, revealing a grey, sickly exterior exactly like the underbelly of some creeping thing. Phlegm bubbled slightly and Jeremiah started foaming at the mouth as barks, hoarse, and loosely syllabled croakings poured forth: "Guuglrog, Ogwhettttt....Shhhhoggggothhhhhh...."

Jeremiah's head clicked in the opposite direction. His eyes widening, larger than his prior outburst; the eyeballs seemed to elongate and darken considerably. "Phlnggewwe?"

I would have ran to the phone on the spot and called you Nora. I wasn't stupid. I knew the sounds, the speech patterns seemed to be like the Deep Ones you've been tracking. I have the ability to recognize, but sadly not translate.

I was too overcome to time or adequately describe this episode. But, it was shorter than the last, and he collapsed, exhibiting both postical paralysis and dyphasia. He said nothing for several minutes as he slouched back against the pillows, arms limp.

"Jeremiah, can you hear me?"

He had closed his eyes and sighed deeply, nodding at my inquiry.

"Jeremiah, what was it you just said? Can you tell me?"

At this my patient opened his eyes slowly, seemed to shake his head or try to. No. Licking his lips he managed a whisper: "N-n-no com-ccompppparable traaanslation."

He closed his eyes again. Seemed to collect himself. Again wriggled his nose and licked his lips. This time, with less staggered speech. "They were a few words I translated off the tablet, which contained instructions...on...On my......," trailing off he closed his eyes and once again relaxed.

"Jeremiah, let's try another direction. Where is the Tablet now? Was this ritual done somewhere on Bay Shore Drive?"

"Yeah-Huh?"

"You were seen nearby screaming. There was a family attacked down there. Then you were picked up on the bridge out to the island. Running around and pulling your hair out and taking off your clothes....." pausing for a moment I thought of his outburst. The words he spoke. "Were the instructions you refer to about calling up something? You are transforming, you said so. And—" I gestured at my own neck by way of illustration. "Did you perhaps get involved with something like a Shoggoth? Was that your intention, Jeremiah?"

Again, the abnormal neck-snap. His head at a painful angle,

his eyes and his face positively elongating. His mouth seemed to widen against nature. The garbled, liquid grumble in his voice left no doubt that he was undergoing the process.

"Something is coming, and happening as we speak..."

"What did you do at the house, Jeremiah? Where is the Tablet Jeremiah?"

"I floated up there. We all float, Dr. Halsey. I was at Bay Shore. I couldn't get back to the Marquis. He abandoned me. I was barred from the temple and the monolith and the Magna Mater cast me out, anyway... though I shouldn't be concerned about Her. Vicious sea-hag. Not like Him. Not like the All-Father. But He lied to me as well. I saw it roll with the tide....It rose and it ate them. I did not know... wasn't sure... it took me years to study and He intended this all along. I supposed and I got it right...."

"Where is the Tablet? How did you float?"

"The ritual wasn't completed. But I tried. I floated the Tablet back home. My home. It's there waiting. But you can't see it. Only the All-Father can. If He wants you to have it, it's there. To be tasted like ice cream. I went to the bridge because I wanted to find the bifurcations in time. In space. The elves would be coming for me soon. As *he* was eating everything below..."

Right. I can hear you now Nora and I half expected my patient to suddenly break into a sing-song, since his croaking voice did take a slightly musical quality to it, and start shrieking, "Make me a sergeant and charge the booze! Make me a sergeant and charge the booze!" I know this is serious, Nora— but I have to agree with him: this can't be happening. If I understand this correctly, this *kid*, this derangement of flesh found a sinister instruction manual, possibly he stole it, but he believes he was given it; by whom? Who is this Marquis? Or, since he, Jeremiah has the affectation of the Curwen name (unless it's not an affectation) AND has tattoos pointing to the Order, does he believe that after Sandy, he was given something, this tablet, by Dagon? And he has since been working to translate it and what....summoned a Shoggoth? To what end? Does he even comprehend what he's done?

I think, despite my many years off the wagon, I may need to jump back on and call for some booze of my own.

"Jeremiah?" He lay again in his post-seizure-noodle state. Staring. Unless he was seizing again.

"Doc." No stuttering. No looking at me. Just head back, eyes on the ceiling. "I'm very tired, and do not feel altogether right....can we talk later?"

"Yes, you can rest, but after one or two more questions."

"Go ahead Dr. Halsey...."

"Is the tablet you spoke of still on Bayshore Drive? And the creature, too?"

"No. Yessshhh, iisshh." He coughed. Clearing away the strangling sound. "Doc...I saw it shamble out of the water where the boats drop off..." His eyes closed once again.

"And this tablet, what you said you found after Sandy? Storms, and Nature as a whole, I don't have to tell you Jeremiah, these things reveal over time what has long been buried and should have never been found."

"Yes. But he gave it to me." His eyes were still closed. "It came from the dealings Obed Marsh had with island people, trading for golden trinkets, idols, and artifact fragments...it sssshaha...ammbled....the Marquis has a tiara...."

"But, where is it?" I didn't need a history lesson.

"Mmmminturn. Housse. I stayed there. Abandoned. Ssshquatted. Minturn Rrroad-oad. It'sss coming. Y'ha-nthlei, the All-Fffather. Mother Hydra....all told to me, when I was taken—" Jeremiah trailed off as another shuddering wracked his body. This time, the seizure caused him to stiffen backwards with such violence he cracked his head back on the headboard. He began screaming a strange conglomeration of sounds beyond the bits of the Deep One language he had previously spoken.

Without waiting for further observations, I immediately shouted out the open door, to the nurses, calling out a Code Grey. I shouldn't have waited. But, anything for you Nora. The tablet was at Minturn Road. I shouldn't imagine there are too many abandoned houses down there. But, with Sandy's influence still dotting areas down there.... Jeremiah Allen is too far gone. The tablet, if it's The Tablet, has been missing for too long and I couldn't risk it disappearing again before you could come for it. His life and my career would be worth the risks. Though, by telling you that, telling everyone that since this is in evidence, I am signing my own retirement papers. Hoka hey.

With black eyes, ready to burst from his skull he shrieked. "IA! IA!" launching himself again pulling at his restraints, thrusting himself in varied directions, I heard what sounded like thick material tear and saw that his right wrist restraint not only came undone but was torn from the bed railing.

Mere seconds after the call, the charge nurse with security only slightly behind made their way in to hold Jeremiah down as another cocktail was injected into his shoulder.

But before the cocktail, Jeremiah lost postural tone, collapsed, and seemed to lose consciousness, signaling a possible syncope response? Security replaced the torn restraint cuffs. After he was secured they went out into the hall to speak with the charge nurse for a report.

I stood in the foyer of Jeremiah's room, washed my hands, splashed water on my face, having already decided upon an executive decision to ring you Nora, my old compatriot.

1144am	STRT FLOOD, NON-TSTM WND DMG OCEAN, NJ	39°56'48.4"N 74°04'21.4"W
8/21/19	INTENSE RAINFALL, 0.15" PER HOUR; STREET FLOODING; POWER LINES DOWN MAKING FOR DANGEROUS CONDITIONS; USE CAUTION BETWEEN W.CENTRAL AVE.-OCEAN TER.	TRAINED SPOTTER

NORA

"Pandemonium on the boardwalk. Good morning. I'm Kemberly Richardson reporting from out here on Barrier Island. Last night, a series of bizarre events clouded the last weeks of summer in Seaside Heights. Police were busy with a gruesome murder across the bay, near Coates Point. Sources tell ABC News that a suspect is in custody. Several tourists had their pets snatched from their yards down around the Route 37 Bridge, both on the Toms River side and over on Pelican Island. Then, two young men were found pulled into a storm grate on the corner of Boulevard and Hamilton, right outside a local nightclub here in Seaside Heights. The rain here isn't helping the situation at all. You can still see the police tape and forensic tent behind me. The scene had to be covered for modesty and to protect the young man's— um— remains. The first young man has yet to be recovered—"

Dr. Danforth crossed the small outer room and popped her head into the inner office of her longtime assistant. "MJ, everything ok? That's pretty loud."

"Sorry, Dr. Danforth."

"You've been my assistant for how long now? You're not my student. You have your own research chops. So Nora, k?"

"Nora. Yes. Something's happening in New Jersey. I saw a strange video pop up in my feed today. Two bennies got themselves into trouble—"

"Bennies?" Nora arched a silver eyebrow. She didn't do it often, but MJ was reverting back to her Jersey Shore lingo that Nora wasn't overly fond of. That and the cursing, which, granted MJ didn't do until she was no longer a student. But, after that trek up to Chesuncook? Nora supposed the experience loosened MJ's tongue. The younger woman was careful and didn't use colloquialisms in front of any of the Armitage Division Board, any students, or really anyone except Nora. If it was MJ's way of working out what had happened with the last holdouts up Maine, then that shouldn't be a problem.

"Yeah. Sorry. You'd call them Summer people. Kids thinking the Jersey Shore and *The Sopranos* is how we all live year round. Whatever. I had just watched their livestream when I turned on the news."

"And?"

"You can't see much in the video. The one posted on Facebook. Just shadows and two kids' close-ups. But what they describe, I don't like. Not after Maine. Social media is blowing up with weird sightings of an alligator?" She sat, scrolling on her phone.

Nora was no luddite. But she prided herself in few things, one of which was she did not use social media. She still had a flip phone and used it only when on location— and only from her car. There was also the whole notion of being able to turn off the device. Nora didn't trust that the blasted thing was truly off unless she was able to actually take out the battery. Thank you Mr. Snowden. Between being tracked by the world's Intelligence and the EMF? Nora never took the thing into a case. The energy interfered in her own abilities to detect and defend. It always struck her as silly, and sometimes life threatening, to carry a device that put out an array of electromagnetic fields on one's person. No wonder the rates of autism and cancer have been on the rise. Anyone with such an exposure, not to mention a contamination of their aura, would pass on such containments to their offspring.

This was one of the reasons for an assistant. Although she hoped MJ wasn't so contaminated. MJ was adapting her own behavior with Nora's guidance and she no longer carried her phone on her body, opting to leave it in her purse or her briefcase, and in a Faraday bag Nora gave the younger woman last Winter Solstice.

"This is bad, Nora. I know where these sightings are. I think —"

MJ's thoughts were cut off by the phone ringing in Nora's office. She held up her finger. "Hold that thought." Not as quickly as she would have liked, Nora went back inside. She was getting older. Chesuncook did take more out of her than she expected. She hated to admit that she was what six years from the half-century mark. Crikey. Five. She would be turning forty-five in October, she realized with some measure of horror, as she reached across the desk and snatched the phone on probably the fifth or sixth ring.

"Dr. Pym Danforth's Office, may I ask who is calling?"

"Nora? This Gilbert."

"Gil? You old goat." She wanted to laugh, but she knew this was no laughing matter. Gilbert Halsey was there: Toms River. The place MJ was already starting a case file for. Nora had trained the younger woman well in the, what seven years since she came to the Armitage Research Division? MJ would be a good second. Like Danforth was to Dyer all those years ago. Like McKenzie was to Armitage and she was to McKenzie. The lines were in place. And MJ proved herself many times before, but especially in Maine.

"Yeah, Nora. Some stuff happening down here. You watch the news at all?"

"My assistant keeps up with the electronic side of things. She's on top of social media too. You still at the Psychiatric Center down there, in Toms River?"

"Why doesn't it ever surprise me you already know...."

"Is it what I think it might be?" Maine surfaced in her mind. The yawning pit. The smell. Maybe she needed something too to help work through *that.* Those pits shouldn't have been there. "It's part of the job, my old friend. Is it a Shoggoth?" She felt a deep, weariness, but drew herself up. No rest. Not until she was dead, she heard her mother say in her mind.

"I believe so. Yes. Undoubtedly."

"So, how'd it get there? From where?" Nora cradled the phone, sat on the edge of her desk, and grabbed her notebook. Extending her arm, with a pop that did not sound good, she grabbed her trusty Phileus. It was a Waterman her mother gave Nora when she graduated, top of Miskatonic's graduating class. Nora always thought of it as her Phineus Bog pen. She never went on a case without it.

But it was out of ink so she tried not to give credence to the superstitious quiffle in her midsection as she grabbed another, non-miraculous pen to take her notes.

"Gil, I sense you may have something to share with me, other than what was broadcast on the news?"

"Indeed, Nora. You see I have a patient who has, in addition to some serious delusions I can go into later, essentially confided in me that he was initiated by Deep One Hybrids in the area, possibly recently as he's currently undergoing a change in room 13C of the Psychiatric Unit. And, on top of that, he claims Dagon gave him a tablet and someone he only identified as the Marquis instructed him, Jeremiah, to conduct a ritual, which appears to have summoned a Shoggoth—"

"Initiated? Did he mention where the tablet was by chance?" Nora paused, writing. "Wait—Gil, repeat his name?"

She spoke aloud as Gilbert did: "Jeremiah D'Bourget Allen Curwen."

But Gilbert added the Curwen. She wasn't familiar with Jeremiah's affectation. Curwen? This didn't bode well. And, there was no way Gilbert Halsey would know who the Marquis D'Bourget was. As if any millennial nitwit harkening toward the path of Joseph Curwen wasn't enough. Add the Marquis to the mix? Of course, it had to be a Shoggoth and the Elder Tablet, too. And after the little bastard stole her chocolates. Those might've helped her in Maine. Or at least helped in the recovery. She was still waiting for her Sacraments to arrive. She supposed she could ask Gil to put in a good word with the university. After all, he was the great grandson of poor Dr. Halsey. The University was still under a kind of debt to his family. Perhaps, if she asked Gil, he could pull a few strings and get the fuddies to loosen up. Psilocybin was on the verge of legalization. They were all about the tablets, scrolls, books and those sort of tangibles. Despite all its vast knowledge, Miskatonic had it's feet in the past. They didn't know about the inner workings of the mind or how to prevent these disasters.

Had they, perhaps given a unit on say psychedelics instead of a mere blip of a mention about the Amazonian dark shamans? Then maybe all that nonsense with MJ's old roommate wouldn't have happened. At this point Miskatonic, was behind the times while The Beckley Foundation, the Hefter Institute, John Hopkins, and the Multidisciplinary Association for Psychedelic Studies were making milestones. *Shit, Dr. Rick Doblin just gave a groundbreaking TEDx Talk on psychedelic therapy a month ago and we're scrambling to set up our own applications?* It almost went without saying, at least for Nora, that science was only just catching up to what the Indigenous peoples across the globe had known for millennia. Clarke was right. Their magic, the essence of their plant knowledge, *was* truly today's science. When Miskatonic was too intent on giving students a foundation in the alternate parallel realms possible in worm-holes and Euclidian theories, they should have had a course on psychedelics. Maybe she should try her own Good Friday Experiment? To some degree the general public was starting to realize they have been lied to about these compounds... Well, had we all been told, had Miskatonic loosened up a single iota, the kid wouldn't have had to steal her gear, even though he never fessed up to having done so. Maybe there wouldn't be a blasted Shoggoth running around Seaside fucking Heights.

Maine's looking nice this time of year.

"You familiar with the lad?"

"You could say that Gil. We'll have a chat about this all, but I've got to get my things in order and head down there. Again, did he say anything about where the Tablet is? It's not in your custody, I take it?"

"No it isn't, but yes he did mention where it might be. This is the same Tablet you've been looking for?"

"Yes. It was taken into custody back in '28, you know with the whole Innsmouth raids, as you know my ancestral namesake was a part of a particular expedition—" Nora yawned. "I'm sorry Gil. It's been a long few weeks."

"We haven't spoken in some time. You fill me in when you're down here, after, ok? But you were saying."

"This is the third time this thing has gone missing. Bloody fish-heads keep dredging it up AND the blasted university's austerity measures. I mean don't get me started about the whole adjunct thing, especially after one got eaten when Professor Neale's Orang Pendek wasn't sleeping like he claimed. I mean how could they? Now the security staff is threatening a strike too. Well, they haven't exactly been up on their end of things since we keep losing rare and fucking dangerous artifacts."

MJ was rubbing off on her. Cursing now are we Ms. Pym?

"Sorry, Gil. I'll fill you in. Apparently it ended up in Toms River?"

"Yeah, this kid, my patient Jeremiah is covered in tattoos, some depicting Deep Ones. He's got some Esoteric Order stuff and what I thought was ritual scarification, but he's also taking on The Look. You know? He did relay to me a bizarre tale. I took notes, but much of it didn't make sense. Though, I was able to piece together that he summoned something."

"A Shoggoth. Another one."

"Unfortunately. What's this about another one?"

Gil had no idea about Chesuncook and she wasn't about to tell him. Not unless there was a bottle of Patron in the situation. Silver only.

"Go ahead Gil. Ignore me."

"Well, we do have some catching up. I couldn't even begin to imagine. But, Jeremiah even blurted out some of the gurgling croaks of the Deep Ones."

"Wonderful. Would you say he's proficient?"

"By no means. He seemed, but it could be the medication so this isn't my medical opinion but the opinion of one who once-upon-a-time worked alongside the great-great-great-great grandniece of the estimable Arthur Gordon Pym. I know enough about their language to have some recognition when I hear it. And that was before the kid sprouted gills."

"Ha ha. Keep reminding me—"

"Well, why take on the name if you didn't want to give reminders?"

Nora laughed. She did miss Gilbert. He was one of her crushes from their school days. It all worked out for the best though. She needed to consider her work and he wasn't into her in that way. A friend would be just fine. After she was through this.

"So, Gil old pal— where is the thing?"

"He said he was squatting in a house on Minturn Road. Why do you need the Tablet? I mean besides for the collection. Hasn't it been spent?"

"You remember the sound of the language, but you forget what you learned in the Innsmouth section of our Physical Anthropology class? I'm surprised at you, Gil. And, I'm not a treasure hunter. I don't risk life and limb just to populate the Special Collections Department."

"I always thought of you as my own Indiana Jones. Too bad you weren't as cute. I've missed you Nora the Explorer."

"Quit while you're ahead, will you?" She couldn't but laugh. "Yeah, the Elder Tablet not only brings forth the Shoggoth, but can reverse the process as well. I doubt Jeremiah studied that portion. The question is how did your patient read the language it was written in?"

"I don't know, Nora. Perhaps his association with the Esoteric Order? But I have not been able to fully explore this in great detail as Jeremiah is very unstable."

"That isn't a surprise, even the most highly skilled practitioners go mad when dealing with items such as this...I'll be down there just as soon as I can put a bag together. I can hear MJ is busy getting her kit together. What time is it now?" Glancing at her watch. "Ok, it's just half-past noon now. Not sure we'll beat the rush. But, if we get on the road in the next hour or two? Even with two driving, it'll take us just under 6 hours to get down. And that's if my assistant wouldn't mind using her vehicle. Mine didn't survive Maine shall we say? The university stopped giving loaners and after that whole business in the bayou, I think my photo has been posted in all the rental agencies north of the Mason-Dixon with a warning *not* to rent anything with wheels to me."

"Don't tell me your car got eaten. It did! Didn't it?"

"Gil. I'm not getting into this with you now. Whenever I get down there, I can come down and interview old Jeremiah? Well...maybe MJ will. Since he probably blames me for getting tossed out of university."

"Do tell?"

"When we have a catch-up. After. Let me put down the beast first. I don't want to even ask, but it's already tearing up downtown

Seaside Heights as well?"

"Unfortunately. Not total devastation. Not yet, but the sightings have started, as I've said. As far as speaking with Jeremiah, but of course, Nora. Anything I can do. If he's not sedated, I'll have to monitor him as he's been having seizures, possibly from the cocktails, but maybe from the transformation."

"Well, he's calling himself Curwen now? Let's hope he's not dabbling with that as well. As if a Shoggoth wasn't enough."

"I didn't want to say, but he did claim to be a magician and he seemed insulted that I thought he meant rabbit-in-the-hat stuff."

"Wonderful. I need a drink."

"Yeah. I might have to go back on the wagon with you, Nora. It was bad. And, I've got the news on mute as we talk. We have a bloody Shoggoth at the boardwalk."

"Great. Let me get your cell so I can get in touch directly." She took down the number. "Sorry we're only getting back in touch like this."

"My thoughts too. I'll be here when your assistant, MJ? When MJ comes down. You owe me a long heart-to-heart. We'll have a beverage."

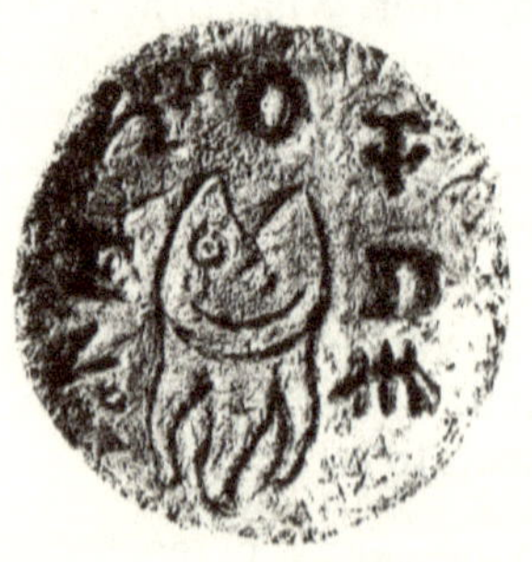

THE MARQUIS

"This is unacsheptable, Marquisssch. You are already treading thin ground with usssh. You have been warned ssseveral timesss. Thish ish your lasst chancsh. The Order hassh no time for your anticsh. Do what needsh to be done."

The shambling figure gave the impression of alluvium. His

form, inveterate, leaning heavily on a stick, not unlike a shillelagh but of what looked like bone. On closer inspection, the Marquis noted it was, of course, driftwood.

This was the annual review he had been putting off for months. It was a nuisance and he was tired of the whole situation. With Asenath McGovern out of the proverbial way, things were supposed to be smoother. But, over the last several years, the Order had truly gotten their priorities inverted. They weren't as keen on world-wide disarray. They didn't want to upset what they saw as a delicate balance. They wanted to sidestep any more business like those bloody raids up north. And, it didn't seem to matter that he had the experience to get things done. True effort, true distinction, mattered for naught.

And things had only worsened since the old harridan's demise. That was an executive decision on the Marquis' part. She had been countermanding his orders. She had been planning on challenging him and with her own grandniece, or whomever the Allen woman was to her; they had both been plotting against him.

And there was the fiasco with the child. The Mason-born offal masquerading as a D'Bourget with the added pretense of a Curwen to make matters truly worse. There was a suspicion, for years after the storm of 2012 that this child had taken something. Something that should have been the Marquis'. Should have returned here to the Temple. Should have been used with caution, but used properly.

With the failure of the ritual, the Marquis knew the Allens hadn't done their part. House the child. Yes. Push the child. Yes. But they had to have been the weakness. *She* kept his Mason birth a secret. *She* had to have known and he could not see this in any way reflecting poorly on him, on his judgement.

What was the old saying about the best kept plans? The Marquis hated erroneous data. He came to the conclusion, rather quickly that something in the child's Mason blood counteracted all the Marquis' plans. Counteracted the application of the ice cream, an innovation thanks to Asenath's smarter, more insightful, more gifted cousins at Maxfield's. It even counteracted the use of the saltes. Both together should have prepared that vessel for the Marquis.

But nothing of the kind happened. The child continued his learning— just enough to shunt him from place to place, but not enough to do anything of true merit. He was supposed to conduct the ritual of ascendance on the spot during the storm. He was under the misguided impression that the ritual he would be uttering would do something to harm the Allens. The Marquis thought it was exceptionally entertaining how the two were at odds. The boy and his foster family. How precious. How delicious. How useful.

But the boy failed.

Because of his own pride, his own arrogance, his own ridiculous affectations and stupidity ,the Marquis remained in this form. A semi-transparent, semi-transformed fish-frog who was still, after what seemed like centuries, under the thumb of Order auditors, like this nauseating lump of detritus here.

To be fair, the audits didn't happen until after Innsmouth failed. But, for the Marquis, who had been used to an independent progression and pursuit of his own agenda, the idea of having to report to anyone was beyond preposterous.

All he had to do was think and he could rearrange this oozing mass at the quantum level. At least he thought he could. Though every time he had tried with the boy, with all manner of things great and small, he failed. Still, he wished he could...

"Marquisssh, do you have anything to add? Do you offer any defenssch? What have you to sssay for yourshelf? Our schourches at the local schanitarium tell usch that the boy hasch been hiding the Elder Tablet. Have you nothing to schay in the matter?"

The Marquis shifted in his seat, leaning back to look at the creature standing in the center of the room. His head felt naked without the coronet. It was another element of this whole situation that was more than he could stomach. He was, perhaps, the only member of their Order who earned and lost a division coronet.

But, his intention was never to take to the seas. Not really. He wasn't overly fond of the idea, but nor was he fond of any necromancy either. How else to continue on, though? Without a proper vessel, which took years to find and mold...only to have it fail? And so terribly...

Now this?

But perhaps Jeremiah's usefulness hadn't expired. Not yet. With this quasi-gelatinous creature before him, an idea began to grow in the Marquis' mind. He might be able to solve a few problems if he could gain the upper hand— over the Order, here regaining his standing in the division and the Order overall— and over the beast the boy called forth? What if the Marquis could take back the Tablet as well? That would be an achievement that would earn him back his crown. That would earn him the right to shape this sector in his own image— as he had been trying to do, with a moderate degree of success for over 200 years.

Perhaps he would direct the Shoggoth to eat this disgusting thing with its driftwood stick first. But that might be too swift an ending for it. Perhaps.

BSA TROOP 38: WEATHER-STATION REPORT #3

<u>Date:</u> August 21, 2019
<u>Time:</u> 4pm
<u>Temperature:</u> 92°
<u>Sky conditions:</u> Overcast; heavy storm, no thunder
<u>Wind:</u> Heavy, gusting at times
<u>Wind Direction:</u> VAR
<u>Wind Speed:</u> lost count of spins; commercial anemometer read 26 miles per hour
<u>Precipitation Type:</u> rain
<u>Precipitation Amount:</u> 0.25"
<u>Additional notes:</u> Litmus test for acid rain: 5

CHARLIE

After logging in the information from the weather-station, Charlie wanted to take a walk down to Van Holten's for one of their bizarre pickle-ices, but it was raining too badly. There was no way he should walk down that far. But he wanted to get something before his parents got home. The house was quiet and he didn't mind walking in the rain.

Despite the temperature, which had fallen a few degrees since earlier in the day, before the rains started, Charlie grabbed his yellow slicker and oilskin Cape Ann Sou'wester. Dad brought them back from a trip up to Salem last year, when Charlie couldn't get out of taking the statewides to be dad's sidekick. It was his fisherman's hat and he sort of looked like the Gorton's Fisherman as he glimpsed himself in the hall mirror as he putting on the sport goggles he usually wore for karate or shooting at the range. Charlie purposefully left his phone at home. He would just go down to the Maxfield's truck down at the corner of Kearney and Boulevard, on the Hook's side of Boulevard.

He'd just get himself a treat and head straight back before anyone noticed. And when dad checked the phone tracker, it would show that Charlie had stayed at home the whole time. It was bad enough that he already had his communication monitored by the government with all their Fusion centers (which he knew were recording everyone's everything), but now dad installed two separate apps to monitor his son's online activities— everything from texting to gaming— and now basically a LoJack system too? So what recourse did he have except to leave the phone at home?

The rain was bad. Bad enough to make him wonder if he shouldn't head back, but by then he had already crossed West Central, so he might as well keep going— at least so he could see if the truck was still there. It wasn't a thunderstorm, so that was something. There were some big puddles. Sort of like little lakes in the dips and hollows in the street or sidewalk. One was standing in Mrs. Heisenberg's front yard. Charlie didn't step in them if he could help it.

Just to the corner to see if the truck was there.

In summers, the Maxfield's truck would sit there until well after sundown. It was their prime season and the little tent they'd have beside the truck, especially if Hook's let them set up in that far corner of the parking lot, would be a great place to sit and enjoy a few scoops to get out of the house. All the better to dispose of any evidence, too...

They were still there!

He crossed Kearney first and then started across Boulevard, when he saw movement out of the corner of his eye. It wasn't a car or anything. No one was on the road really. There was something sticking out of the storm drain at the corner, just opposite the Maxfield's truck, which looked like they were starting to pack up for the afternoon. Nope. The whatever it was could wait. Ice-cream first.

"You're just in time, kiddo." The weird, bulbous guy in the window said, smiling a smile with way too many teeth. Charlie thought of a piranha. And he was sure the guy's skin was a bit green around the edges. Maybe it was some tattoo or something.

"Got anything new?"

"We have some Captain Nemo's Revenge. It's got chocolate squid bits."

"Give me a two scoops in a waffle bowl. You keeping the tent up for a bit?"

"Yeah, kid. For a bit. We're closing in half an hour. Storm's getting bad. They say it's from that volcano. Over in Iceland. Can you believe that shit? Sorry–" The guy coughed a little in a slightly nauseating way, making a bit of a gollum sound.

Dude did remind Charlie of that creepy little blighter from those awful Peter Jackson films. Now, there was a guy who had no clue about how to get Tolkien right. Well, Charlie hoped gollum here didn't give him anything contagious. It would be his luck to get sick in the last weeks of summer vacation.

Guy cleared his throat again. "Can you believe it? Volcano all the way over there upsetting our beautiful heat wave over here?"

"It's science. It happens whether you believe it or not."

The guy tilted his head to the side and blinked a pair of overly large eyes that were almost black. Kind of like a shark's.

Walking all the way across town to Van Holten's didn't seem so bad.

"You bein' a smart-ass?"

"No. Just logical. A volcano across the Atlantic Ocean spewing dust and debris into the atmosphere will cause a fluctuation in weather patterns, especially when taking into account that things like air flow. You do know that the air we're breathing now has travelled and will continue to travel across the planet, right? Science isn't like the Easter Bunny or God. It happens regardless of belief. And, unlike our current administration's inability to comprehend that fact, weather patterns and climate are a particular branch of science that is, as far as I'm concerned, more important to human survival than petty belief. Can I have my ice cream now?"

"Yeah, you little smart ass. That'll be three-fifty. You're too young to be talkin' like that. It might get you in trouble. Wait over there for your ice cream."

Charlie hated adults who thought they were smarter than he was, especially when he knew they were dumber than a bag of igneous rock. And there seemed to be a plague of such things in the world— not just in New Jersey.

The guy gave him two skimpy scoops in a waffle bowl that was cracked along one side, so as he ate, it dripped. Still. It was better than no ice cream. Charlie didn't want to sit. The single cafeteria-styled table was puddled with water from where the tent had sprung a leak. As if to tell Charlie to piss off, the guy shut the truck window. So Charlie stood there, eating his ice cream, looking up and down the semi-desolate street.

He saw movement again from that storm drain he had forgotten about. He wasn't sure what he was looking at. It was a small black mass about the size of a volley ball. If it wasn't so large, and so roundish, he would have thought it was maybe a kitten that had gotten washed down the block. He wasn't overly fond of cats, but if one was about to drown in a storm drain, Charlie would certainly go help it. Wasn't there a merit badge for animal rescue?

But, as he finished his leaky waffle bowl, he could see that it wasn't an animal. Though it was moving against the flash floods tearing down the gutter on Boulevard. He briefly wondered if he shouldn't go check it out. He looked down at his slicker and remembered what happened to poor Georgie. He was too young to read the book, but he wasn't too young to sneak into the back of the Marquee Cinemas two years ago. He and EJ will probably do the same thing when part two comes out in the fall.

There was something there. He resolved to cross near enough to check it out, but keep some distance just in case it was some diseased terrier or whatever. He didn't want any blob sort of nonsense happening, especially after those bennies from Staten Island got themselves smashed by a semi, eaten by an alligator (which is what EJ said), or whatever last night. Charlie was surprised that after *that* the street was so empty. He supposed the news cycle was so quick now that two teens getting demolished on a street corner in Seaside Heights didn't come close to the idea of a near war with Iran or Turkey, the latest allegations about whateverthehell, or about the dust-cloud from Icelandic volcanoes halting air-traffic across the North Atlantic and most of Europe. The last news van had left probably around lunch-time and the police had finished their work in the wee hours of the morning. It wouldn't do for there to be an active crime scene a few blocks up from the boardwalk during the summer season. Sort of reminded him of that Mayor in *Jaws*. Who cared if there was an alligator in the storm drains or a random tractor trailer driven by a serial killer aiming for kids partying the summer away? As long as the summer people didn't leave...

Finishing the last of his ice cream, he dumped the soggy, mess of a waffle bowl and wiped his hands across the front of his slicker. It was wet and it was still pouring. So the rain would wash it clean. Pulling his Sou'wester down snugly, he went into the tempest that seemed to be getting worse instead of better. Crossing quickly, he went to see what was what.

223 MINTURN ROAD, TOMS RIVER

"Thank you for meeting us, Officer Cortez? I'm Dr. Danforth and this is my assistant, Ms. Berkana," Nora extended a hand to the officer, shouting over the downpour. Nora and MJ had just pulled MJ's 1974 Volkswagen bus behind the police cruiser parked as close to the home on Minturn as possible.

The middle-aged officer had been standing outside the boarded up front door, finishing a cigarette while she waited to show these academic massholes where that nutbar had been holed up. Cortez was at least happy the house still had a roof over the porch. Even though it was a bit leaky, it was better than standing in the rain.

"You drive down from Boston in that thing?" Officer Cortez nodded toward the car, in it's violent purple splendor. MJ wasn't happy about driving all this way in her father's classic, but there was no way Nora would be loaned a car anytime soon and the doctor had promised any car issues were on her dime, not MJ's. Plus she paid for gas and was using her own EZ-Pass. MJ thought the bus was making a bit of a homecoming, seeing how she had grown up in this neighborhood. It was a horror to drive in Arkham, but Nora needed room for the supplies. The two hadn't stopped at the motel yet.

"Arkham."

"What's that?" Drag. Exhale. Almost in their faces.

"We're from Arkham. I'm the Director of the Armitage Research Division with Miskatonic's Orne Library and this is my research assistant."

"Yup. You said. Still. Isn't that what I asked?"

"Arkham is further north than Boston. We drove from there." MJ and Nora exchanged glances, trying to remain calm. The officer didn't need to be standing here in the rain to baby-sit a few eggheads — as they were sure the officer thought of them. Either that or worse.

"Arkham, Boston. Same diff. You want in here or what?"

"Yes, Officer. That would be most appreciated."

"Yup. Watch your footing. Some loose boards here."

The officer sliced the door-seal with a multi-tool, unlocked the padlock that seemed to have been recently installed, and allowed them both to enter.

"Has anything been removed from the premises?"

"Not yet, Doc. We got word from On High to leave things as is. The kid wasn't arrested, so this isn't part of a crime scene. But, we sealed it up like we were instructed."

"Thank you Officer Cortez."

The moment Nora stepped over the threshold she could taste the energy at play here. It was clear that there had been some layers to the history of this place, beyond a simple deranged squatter. As she stepped over the broken bit of flooring, what she suspected might have been a booby trap at some point, she touched the doorframe. A few flashes came to mind.

Jeremiah covered in what looked like mud, kneeling in the center of the room. A chalk outline on the floor of sigils and twisting shapes peeping out from beneath him. His hair coiling like tentacles. Liquid burblings spilled from his mouth.

But this was no Deep One language that the boy spoke. Not then. Not in that flash. It was nonsense. He was play-acting.

But why did she get the pull on her mind? Why did she feel—

"Doc, you going in or are we staying out?" Officer Cortez interrupted.

MJ had been lagging behind. She found herself more than distracted at the sight of the house. To think that *this* is where Jeremiah had ended up? She should have done something to help. She had already confided in Nora that she felt some responsibility about this whole situation. If she hadn't agreed with Jaimie, if they both hadn't told Jeremiah that lines had been crossed irrevocably, then perhaps he wouldn't have would up in the sanitarium and perhaps he wouldn't have dabbled in such darkness. Nora had told her that for that matter, it was her fault too since she was stupid about leaving her truffles in her desk. Nora said had she kept them home, instead of using them at work to microdose, then Jeremiah wouldn't have been booted that first time. BUT, ultimately it was all Jeremiah's doing and neither MJ nor Nora were to blame for his actions.

MJ tapped the Officer on the shoulder to give Nora the time she needed to do the laying-on-of-hands part of the investigation. Reading the place was always the first step and MJ kicked herself for not keeping the Officer back.

"Officer Cortez, could you tell me about the address? The history? Anything you can while Dr. Danforth begins her work? She usually walks the locale solo for a little bit. It gives her a better picture of the ins-outs-and-what-have-yous." MJ was more than familiar with the Minturn Witch and had even heard that the old woman had died. Yet, there were holes in her knowledge of the site. She had learned a little from online research, but needed to see what information the officer knew.

"What? Like Will Graham?" Officer Cortez laughed, making a sucking sound. "How about a nice Chianti? Any fava beans? Ha." And, MJ couldn't believe, but the stocky but incredibly tall female cop actually slapped her knee.

She wanted to smile, but instead kept it deadpan. "Not exactly, but we think of the Armitage Research Division more like Scully and Mulder."

Cortez looked at her. Blinked a few times and then let out a raucous laugh that made tears stand out in her brown eyes. "Figures. Scully. Oh boy. She kinda looks like her. But without the red hair." She kept laughing. "Can I ask? How old is she? But as chick-to-chick. I mean. She can't be much older than I am. But her hair... I mean..." The officer's humor faltered.

"Premature greying runs in her family...?" MJ suddenly did not like Officer Cortez. She couldn't tell the taller woman that the shit both of them had seen would turn anyone's hair white. And

Nora's hair was so white in places it was silver. When MJ had started working with Dr. Danforth, the woman's hair was black. Then, as their work progressed over the next seven years, it slowly started in streaks, not unlike Polgara from the David Eddings books MJ used to read when she was a kid. Then, after Louisiana it went a steely grey, pretty much in one swoop. After Maine? White. "So, Officer Cortez, tell me about 223 Minturn Road. Is there any history here?"

Officer Cortez stepped back a few short paces, almost to the edge of the porch, motioned with a cigarette, and proceeded to light up when MJ nodded that she didn't mind.

"Well. This is a funny place. Back a bit, maybe ten years ago? Wait, longer. Before Sandy. There was an old woman lived here. See I grew up a few blocks down. I remember the old bat. Kids used to tease her. We called her the—"

"Minturn Witch."

"How'd you know that?" Drag. Puff.

"I grew up over on Sheridan."

"You're not from Boston, then?"

Arkham! "No, officer. New Jersey born and raised."

"Berkana. Weird name."

Thanks. "It's an old name. Norse for Birch. You know, the tree?"

"Yeah... no. I mean. I know the name. You any relation to Thomas Berkana?"

"Yes. He was my father."

"Why didn't you say your dad was on the job? That he was line of duty no less." Officer Cortez extended her hand to MJ, took the smaller woman's hand in her own, and held it quietly for a moment. "I met your dad a few times. He worked with my uncle on Barrier Island for a bit. He was a good cop."

"Thank you." She swallowed back the lump that seemed to grow. It had been there for a good stretch of the ride down here, just thinking about Jeremiah, but now with memories of dad on top of everything? Ok. She had to focus her shit. Nora was counting on her. "So, Officer Cortez "

"Cindy. Call me Cindy. So, the house. You know about the Minturn Witch and that she was obsessed with Halloween decorations."

"What happened to her? I was away at school during Sandy. Was this house damaged at all?"

"Sure. Whole block was fucked. Still has places that Obama forgot about. But, the Witch? She disappeared right around Sandy, so we all thought— the town I mean, her family too— that she maybe didn't evacuate. She was housebound and maybe she didn't get to a shelter. She was unaccounted for. And while the house didn't wash away, this whole place was under water pretty much." Cortez finished her cigarette and flicked the butt into a localized waterfall cascading off the porch roof. She sighed, eyeballing the house when she noted Nora kneeling in the center of the room, hands flat on the floor. "What the fuck is she doing?"

"Investigating. So, tell me about Mrs. McGovern?"

"So you knew her?"

"No. I told you. I was at school when she went missing. You were saying?"

"Yeah. The house was still here, damaged, but not enough to tear down I guess. Thing is. McGovern's nephew came down from upstate. He inherited from the old lady I guess. He snapped up the house next door, too. Tore that fucker down, rebuilt it from the ground up. But this one? He just fixed it and rented it out. That kid, the one who squatted here, had lived here for a time. Dunno how long. But, before he went batshit, he had been living here.

"Funny thing though. The nephew, he lived next door with his wife and three girls. He was just as much a Halloween nut as his aunt. He used to have some business. Maybe he still does, but he moved and I don't know. But, he made these figurines and shit. You know that bookshop across on Barrier Island?"

"Bookshop?"

"Yeah. Freaky one. Down by the boardwalk." Cortez pointed over her shoulder pointedly as though that would tell MJ the exact locale of said freaky bookshop. "Sort of a theme? Like it's supposed to be of real shit, you know? Stuff from legends. Like the Fiji mermaid. Dude made a bunch of the things. Went all out. Jersey Devil, alien abductions, monkey's paw, that kind of shit. Fucking shopkeeper had some problem. Got rid of a mess of his stuff. A real shame. I really like his stuff. My girlfriend too. She's also obsessed with Halloween, the movie. So for her birthday a few years ago, I bought her this Halloween themed monthly mail-order thing that this guy does from his online shop. Every month you get these statues. Small ones, but really detailed, unique shit. He ran a business out of his back porch or something. Casting and painting these things. I swear. She got this little Jason from the movie that was really neat, but looked like candy. Like a fucking gummy bear or something. She still has them of course. But, anyway. Dude made these things out of his house. Over there." She pointed over MJ's shoulder to another house, also boarded up in places.

"I take it he's no longer here?"

"I'm getting to that. It's good. So, dude worked with an assistant. Guy was a bit strange. Not as strange as his boss, get me. But you've got to be a little weird to have a business that sells gummy looking slasher film characters, right? Anyway. You ever hear of squatchin?"

As if she didn't take two semesters of Professor Neal's Cryptozoology? But she looked quizzically and played the dumb-redhead.

"Looking for Sasquatch." Cortez waited for a punchline. But, MJ just nodded, straight-faced. "Well, this guy went what he called Wooga-hunting. Guy was a drinking buddy of my brother's. Can't remember his name. Wooga-hunter, not my brother." Another knee-slapper. "Well, guy went missing and I was part of the initial investigation. My brother was one of the last folks in town to see the guy. He was planning to finally, as he put it, get some answers."

"To what?"

"What he called the Elusive Wooga and the Mystery of Honey Brown."

In addition to the undergraduate work with Professor Neal, MJ had taken an advanced seminar at the graduate level. She had never heard of a fucking Woogah or Honey Brown. Fucking piney nutjobs.

"Anyway, he went missing off Route 72, over by the old Cedar Bridge Tavern, the site of our very own highwaymen. But that's another story."

"So what about the nephew. Did he go missing as well?"

"No no no. He didn't go in for drinking Jagermeister and running around the woods on a monster-hunt. Dude made monsters for fun and for a business, but he had his shit together. Although, like I said he did rent to Mr. Nutbar. The kid who went cracker-jacks the other night. Right when that other guy got chomped by whateverthefuck across the canal. But, the Halloween guy. He and his family skedaddled after they found his aunt."

"Mrs. McGovern was ok?"

"No ma'am. She wasn't. Family moves in after they rebuilt. So let's say, 2013-2014? Lives there for a bit. Rents to nutterbutters maybe two years ago? Three? Whatever. Nutters leaves. Gets evicted. Committed. Whatever. Then, Mr. Halloween's girls started hearing sounds in the house. He thought his taste in movies and his job was giving the kids nightmares. But, then the other two girls start hearing stuff. Moans. Groans. Voices. Then the wife does. Everyone's hearing shit except Mr. Halloween. He even goes so far as to hire some paranormal investigation group. You know, that dude with the pony tail that worked with the guy with that haunted museum up in New England? Again. My girl watches all that shit. All those shows. I personally think it's bullshit, but whatever. Either way. This group comes down and they don't find anything paranormal. The team got their hands on ground penetrating radar and they go over this whole place. What do you think they find? Right there. In the middle of the yard between this place and the rebuilt place, right where that gazebo is— they find something was buried there. Next few days, guy rents a backhoe and whaddya know. He turns up his aunt's body. Buried in the yard."

"Mrs. McGovern was murdered?"

"Seems so. Dismembered too. Found bits of her all over the yard actually. Found a trunk with her clothes in it too. Suitcase I think, with her clothes and torso. Kinda like those bodies they found a while back in the canal down in Asbury Park."

"I take it nothing came of it? No arrests?"

Officer Cortez shook her head and started on her third cigarette. MJ felt sick.

"Guy up and leaves with the whole fam of course. But—"

Just then Nora came to the rescue. She nodded at MJ. "We're good to go, MJ. Officer Cortez, thank you for your assistance. Can you direct us to the Toms River Psychiatric Unit?"

"Over on 37. I can take you—"

"No need," MJ interjected. "I know the place. My mother worked there for a few years before her time at Community. She was a nurse."

"I apologize, MJ. I keep forgetting you're from the area."

MJ nodded.

"Thank you, Officer Cortez for your help."

"No problemo. Call if you need anything." She handed Nora a card with her information just as a call came over the walkie.

"Calling all units. Calling all units. Attack on Boulevard. Possible animal attack. Multiple injuries. Possible DOA—"

As the officer ran to her patrol car, Nora turned to her assistant. "Do you mind taking me to the hotel? I have to prepare before facing the creature, as horrible as that sounds. We also need quite a bit of salt. We passed a few box stores on the way. We need to stop and get a few more things. Would you mind interviewing Mr. Allen yourself? I did say my presence might not go over well, you know..."

"No problem, Nora. Motel is on the way. Don't cringe though. It's a bit hinky. There aren't many rooms in this area at this time of year."

"No worries. We'll be fine. You worried about me? You remember the shack in the woods behind Myrtles Plantation? What's a little hink for an old chick like moi?" Nora laughed and readjusted her hair, pulling down her bun, twisting it tighter, securing it with what looked like a miniature knitting needle, silver, inlaid with, at a glance what looked like simple black enamel-work. But, MJ took comfort that already Nora was protecting herself. The black scroll-work along the hairpin was a protective spell that MJ herself was learning the mastery of. Nora didn't take that much comfort in such things, but after Maine, she didn't want any complacency.

Every bit would help.

THE MONOLITH

At least the steps! If he could at *least* get to the steps, perhaps the thing couldn't follow him. Not up there. It was protected. Father Dagon wouldn't permit it...would He?

The Marquis had to try. The rains pelted down as he dashed down Boulevard toward Hiering. These rains were different though, like the creature. They stung his skin, got into his eyes and made his vision shift, burningly so. Great blisters appeared on his hands, across his frills, blistering his gill slits. It felt like he was aflame. Agony.

In the years since the devastation of Hurricane Sandy, a CVS had been built right beside the monolith. The back wall of the store was a mere foot from the grand staircase that coiled its way around the monument to Father Dagon and Mother Hydra. Of course, the true size and shape of it was hidden, as was Their temple and all Their places of true importance.

But, the Marquis might try to escape the creature there. Or, use the higher ground to do battle. His attempts by the beach were wholly unsuccessful. The creature tore its way up from the water a roiling mass wholly unlike any Shoggoth the Marquis had hitherto encountered.

Granted, that wasn't many. But, he knew them to be of a certain condition. This one though seemed to be more than its brethren. More than the simple, oozing beast of burden. Not only did it have some prescience, moving in anticipation of the Marquis' own actions, but it was much larger than it should be. The color was strange. As the rain hit it, it seemed to change, roil, expand. He could have sworn, in the dimming light, the sun not yet down but the sky dark with storm, that the creature shed a portion of itself. That couldn't have been right. It must have been a trick of the rain, the gloaming, the sting in his eyes.

And, it wasn't just eating either... at least not mindlessly. Perhaps at first, before the rains came. Then it seemed to take to ground, disappearing during the day into the tunnels beneath the town. Tunnels which the Marquis had used in his old highwayman days. He worked for a time with the Order's northern kin who had made such spectacular tunnels in New York City to expand the old smuggling tunnels he had used in his youth. Especially after Sandy had damaged so much. There had been a series of tunnels running from the channel at Barnegat Lighthouse. He had used them, along with other smugglers, for ages. But, with help of the those bizarre Marsh descendants in New York, he had been able to rebuild some of the damaged tunnels. Those tunnels, what he thought of as his tunnels, had been the backbone extending up Barrier Island directly beneath Shore Road and Route 35, beneath the bay, where they branched off, some terminating up near the Toms River Municipal Courthouse. Others stretched beyond to the old Geigy site. He was happy now that they had left the Oyster Creek station alone. The last thing the Marquis wanted was a Shoggoth inhabiting a decommissioned nuclear power station.

The Shoggoth knew about the tunnels. How could it though? It had no master.

The child was tucked away in the sanitarium. The whereabouts of the Elder Tablet was unknown. But, when the Marquis tried to hone in and search using the old alchemical methods, something was blocking him, preventing him from seeing where the Tablet was. Though he did employ a pendulum to help fine-tune his search. Perhaps that was it. Maybe his pomposity had been the thing. Using a device instead of himself? He felt shame, for the first time in decades.

As he had been puzzling over how to proceed, what technique to use to locate the Tablet, he heard a prolonged commotion coming up from the beach, something beyond the miscreant summer folk. Over the years, the Marquis was able to tune out the noise and their effluvia. He had been in his workshop in the back room of the temple and what he had thought was just another of their "block parties" suddenly turned into an unremitting sound. There were screams, yes. There was the sound of rain, which had started earlier that day.

Then he heard what he feared— and before he could locate the Tablet!

TEKELILITAKKELI-TEKELILILILI-TAKKKELLLIII....

He gathered himself and went to meet it amidst its feast. Despite the rain, there were still summer folk gathering on the boardwalk and near the ocean. Nothing the Marquis did made a bit of difference. No spell. No summoning. Nothing. So, he ran. Back. He tried to get to the temple, but it had him cornered.

They did. Two of them.

One of the creatures bubbled up from the boardwalk, rolling like something out of his childhood nightmares— things his power and his station had long since buried. The Marquis D'Bourget did not have scary dreams. Little frightened him. What he saw now did.

At one end of the block, its back to the ocean which itself was more than a block away, was the creature he had met at the boardwalk. It seemed to fill the space between the buildings on either side of the road. This was easily larger than any Shoggoth he had ever heard tell of. The surface was a boiling mass of eyes, teeth, proboscides, and pseudopodia. Each mouth that surfaced reverberated with its mocking, acidulous cry:

TEKELILITAKKELI-TEKELILILILI-TAKKKELLLIII....

Then it wasn't merely the chorus from the creature about 100 yards off, rippling toward him. It was a cacophony that also came from *behind him.*

Not wanting to turn his back to the first one, he had to see. There behind him was another, not nearly as large. It was an identical copy, but no larger than he was. It repositioned itself and he was looking at a blurry, billowy copy of himself. It stood just outside the temple. At the very doorstep!

The only thought in his mind was to try again, try the spell again on the monolith. He could not fathom that these creatures could climb, at least not those stairs. He turned again, trying to still and occlude his mind. Since the creature exhibited a degree of forethought he couldn't comprehend, he fixed an image in his mind of a blank sheet of paper as he ran down a rivulet of the stinging water between the houses between the Carteret and Sampson avenues. He did not look back, and kept moving a head. To the CVS. And then, to the steps of the monolith.

Up. Around. Up. Around. Up. Stumble. Up and up and up.

At the top, the great seal was chipped, cracked, but remained true. As did the gateway. The Marquis stood, back to the gateway and he used his last mustering.

He did not know it would be his last breath:

UAAAH Y'AI'NG'NGAH SHOG-GOTH FK'EE-FK'GLEB HA'F'AI THRODOGIAAAAUAAAH Y'AI'NG'NGAH SHOG-GOTHFK'EE-FK'GLEBHA'F'AITHRODOG IAIAAAAUAAAH-NGAH SHOG-GOTHFK'EEFK'GLEBHA'F'AITHRODOGIAIAAAAAAAAAA

The Marquis could also not fathom the precipitous distention that rose up on first one, then two, then all sides of the monolith, engulfing it completely in a wall of eyes, teeth, and slavering mouths.

Nor could he fathom that all his efforts would always and forever be useless without the power of The Elder Tablet.

MJ could't believe her ears. "What do you mean exactly, that he escaped?"

"I mean exactly what I said, ma'am. Jeremiah Allen is no longer a patient at the Toms River Psychiatric Unit."

MJ was glad Nora was back at the motel taking a ritual bath with holy water, helichrysum, Cascarilla powder, Abramelin oil, lots of basil, and a dash of asafœtida. Otherwise the woman would reach across the narrow counter and grab this tub of useless flesh by his elephant-print scrubs and slap that smirk off his face.

"So, what did you do exactly? Open the door and let him leave? Have you called the police? Or are you hoping he gets returned like a lost shoe?"

"Now, ma'am, there's no reason to be hostile. I take exception to your tone."

"Is Dr. Halsey here? I need to speak with Dr. Halsey."

"Halsey went home for the evening—"

"Again, what's being done regarding your escaped patient?"

"We have his description and a bulletin circulating, but I think the police have been more than a little busy across in Seaside. Things are getting a bit weird down there. No, offense, ma'am. But my shift is over in a few moments. Is there anything else I can help you with here?"

"Nothing-whatsoever. I'll be putting in a good word with Dr. Halsey on your behalf. Maybe they'll give you a commendation or a bonus for losing another warm body. Cheers."

CHARLIE

"Charlie! Where the fuck are you?"

The moment Charlie closed the patio doors, having come around the back of the house when he saw his father's car back in the driveway, he knew he shouldn't have gone out earlier. Ice cream wasn't worth an ass beating. At least the rain had stopped. Well, sort of. It wasn't a monsoon any more. So that was something. Had it stopped, the water might have washed it off him. He did walk back in some of those mini-lakes. He stopped and stomped around in Mrs. Heisenberg's front lawn.

But he couldn't get it off. The muck.

"Did you go out of the fucking house, man? What did I tell you? I didn't raise you to be stupid. Come on. You're better than this."

Charlie stood there, at the back porch, dripping on his mother's new white and grey checkered rug. He couldn't help but think it was the ugliest rug he had ever seen. It smelled like an old sheepdog. Now, it would be a wet sheepdog. With a nice stain about the shape and color of that thing he had seen poking its appendage at him from the sewer grate. He didn't touch it, but there was a black ichor around it, sort of like oil, but more like squid ink since it stained his shoes and seemed to coat them. But it wasn't just squid ink because no amount of stomping or splashing could get it to come off.

He also couldn't help but think of the blob. He really wanted his feet to be there when he took off his shoes. He knew as his father stood there, screaming his bearded face purple, Charlie couldn't say: "Can it Dad while I check to see if my feet are intact?"

So he stood there, in his yellow slicker and his Sou'wester. Sport goggles fogging to the point that he could no longer see his father. He could still feel his toes. They were there. He was certain of it.

His stomach promptly flipped. Flopped. Then he vomited a sputum of old Captain Nemo's Revenge on mom's carpet. Now it was white, grey, black, and variegated browns.

D4224: "David-4-2-2-4. Central. Come in central."

DISPATCH: "D4224. This is Central. Go ahead."

D4224: "I need help, Central. Send the fucking calvary, Central. NOW! I need the fucking marines or something."

DISPATCH: "Language D4224. You need a verbal? What's going on?"

D4224: "I'll fucking take it. It'll mean I'd be alive to get it. I'm down at Carteret and Boulevard. At least I think that's where I am. There's something down the road. Half the block is gone. Everything from " (Inaudible) " to Boulevard is fucking gone. It's like—" (Inaudible)

DISPATCH: "D4224, come in D4224. Units are en route. The area needs to be staged?"

D4224: "10-4 Central. We've got power lines down and something's— I don't know what's going on. It's—" (Interference) "-ie. It's gone. Need all units. EMS. Fire. Men-in-fucking-black. Don't know here. I don't know what I'm—" (Inaudible) " looking at Central. I just saw some kid, naked as a jaybird, covered in tattoos. Scrawny white kid with dreads. This *thing...* it's no animal, Central. Nothing I've ever seen—"(Inaudible; interference)

DISPATCH: "EMS is en route D4224. Are there casualties?"

D4224: "Fucking kid. He stood there!" (Interference) "aiming at it. Waving his arms like he was telling it what to do! Part of it... part of it..." (Inaudible)

DISPATCH: "You're breaking up D4224. Come in D4224?"

D4224: "I'm here. Part of it came away. It looked like the kid, Central! It went up to him like... he was going...." (Inaudible) "—hugged it. And it tore his fucking head off."

At least in Maine, the creatures hadn't grown, hadn't evolved, hadn't become like this. It was bigger than her mind could hold. But, she would do what needed doing. She was prepared and when MJ met her back at the motel, Nora had insisted that MJ also prepare herself. Although, MJ didn't sit meditating in the tub for as long as Nora had done.

This would have been a perfect time to make use of a truffle. It would focus her mind. *Jeremiah.* MJ was near hysterics— which was the *only* time MJ had ever cried, much less gotten anywhere near such a state in all their years together, both as mentor and friend. MJ was not a woman who turned toward anything approaching such agitation or fatuousness.

But, this was MJ's friend, her childhood companion, her roommate. Despite his failings— and there were so many— Jeremiah Allen was MJ's family. And, from all accounts he had escaped to meet his creature and since he was a total incompetent, there would be zero chance in his success.

The idea of him subjugating or even battling the creature? Futile. Even were he to still possess the Elder Tablet, which he most certainly did not.

She needed a staging area.

"MJ. Where did you grow up? Exactly."

"Buchanan. Well, Sheridan, but the two streets are back-to-back and Jeremiah's house, where I spent a lot of time, is on Buchanan. Was."

"Show me where." Nora tapped MJ's phone as the two woman sat on the edge of one of the shabby twin beds in the threadbare little room they had been able to get at the Shore Motel. It was a double and a smoking room, so at least Nora was able to fumigate the place with blue sage and palo santo.

Before MJ came back with the news about Jeremiah's flight, Nora had taken the precaution to write the tablet phonetically in the reverse to draw the Shoggoth back, to unmake it, on a piece of flash paper Nora always kept in her kit bag. Should she be unable to complete the spell, should the beast get the better of her, Nora needed to know that MJ would be able to complete the task. While MJ could read some of the Deep One's tongue, she wasn't proficient enough to pronounce it. Not yet.

This would be a final option. Her mother always taught her to have at least three back-ups, three alternatives. So Nora had three.

MJ pointed out her old house. It would do nicely. Near to the water. And a circle already there, physically. It might make the application easier. Back-up number two was back in play with the rain having stopped.

They would have to get there and set up.

SHERIDAN AVENUE PARK, TOMS RIVER

The sun had long since sunk behind them. The sky wasn't yet fully dark, but there was enough light to lay the salt circle. It wasn't necessary to circumvent the entire park. The salt would have no effect on the Shoggoth.

But it might protect them. Nora decided the first course was to call on the ancient powers of protection. If the Tablet was inside the circle with them, then the women could keep it beyond the reach of the creature. The protection would also prevent either of them from succumbing or being supplanted by the creature.

What Nora did decide was to cover the ring of the park with an old favorite of hers. It saved them in the bayou. It was portable, a bit smelly, but a little went a really long way. Greek fire. The Orne had the original Assyrian recipe. It wouldn't be the only thing the Assyrians would help her with tonight. The Greek fire might not kill the creature, but it would help contain it.

It might kill any offshoots though. From what they were hearing, between the repeated animal attacks reported on the news and the murmurings across town, more than one something had been sighted across the area between Seaside Heights and part of Toms River.

Nora hoped that the Tablet would contain and unmake the main creature. Perhaps, taking a leaf from the old Hammer movies of her childhood? Prevail over the master, the spawn will likewise be obliterated. She hoped.

"Nora, we're ready." MJ finished the last touch on their impromptu altar by lighting a small pile of charcoal she had left-over from a camping trip at Echo Lake that she had gone on a few weeks earlier with Jaimie. The two women had left Arkham so quickly, MJ didn't have a chance to empty the camping gear from the van. She still had much of the camp kitchen she and Jaimie had loved using. She hoped he wouldn't mind her turning his grandmother's dutch oven into a cauldron. She liberally sprinkled the smoldering coals with a mixture of white sage, copal, dragonsblood, palo santo, rosemary, and, since they were outside, a large handful of asafœtida.

As Nora said. Every little bit helps.

MJ kept the flares away from the grill, but close enough to light and throw at a moment's notice.

Nora closed the salt circle around where the women took position— on a decrepit basketball court almost exactly in the center of the park just across from MJ's childhood home. They had the added good fortune that the park was a circle at the center of a seven-way crossroads.

Nora wasn't one to believe in providence. Not really.... but still... She thanked the Goddess and both women set to work. In unison, they both began the spell.

"Ban! Ban! Ban!
A Barrier that none can pass,
A Barrier of the Gods that Shall not be broken!
A Barrier of Heaven and Earth that None Can Change!
A Barrier which no God may Annul—no god, nor man can loose,
A Snare set for Evil, without escape,
A Net whence no Evil can light upon, no ill will can taint or infect,
None with Evil Intent Shall Pass this Boundary!
Whether it be Evil Spirit or Evil Fiend,
Demon or Phantom,
Shoggoth or Nightgaunt,
Mi-go or Pestilence,
Be it that which may do harm in any form or fashion,
It Shall Not Pass!
May the Great Gods Entrap it,

May the Great Gods Curse it,
May the Great Gods Snare it,
Should this barrier be tested,
Whatever which bloweth in at the threshold and hinge,
Or which forceth a way through bar and latch,
Like water, may the Great Gods pour it out,
Like a goblet, may They dash it to pieces,
Like a tile, may They break it,
Or which Evil passeth over the wall
Its wing may They cut off,
Or which Evil lieth in a chamber
Its throat may They cut,
Or which ill will looketh in at a side chamber,
Its face may They Smite,
Or which wickedness muttereth in a chamber,
Its mouth may They shut,
Or which Fiend roameth loose in an upper chamber,
With a basin without opening may They cover it,
Or which shadow Darkens the Dawn
At Dawn to a Place of Sunrise May They take it."

MJ would continue in an unbroken volley as Nora used the Tablet to first summon and then unmake the creature. Should Nora fall, MJ already had the flash paper with the pronunciation, to be consumed by the ritual fire the moment it was no longer needed.

Passing the Elder Tablet over the ritual smoke, as MJ kept chanting while tending the fire, flares at arm's length, Nora began the first wave and started the summoning.

The language physically hurt her to utter. It left a kind of burn across her soul. Something no ritual bath could remove. She felt it in the tips of her hair and the roots of her toes. She kept speaking the foul tongue as she felt the ground shudder. The air seemed to thicken and a pulsating sound rose up from the shore about fifty yards to the south. A rolling, oscillation climbed up, consuming all the houses, cars, trees in the space between. Nora couldn't think about how many people might have been at home watching late-night tele.

It was there with its preposterous cry. Mocking. Chiding. Screeching across her mind.

"Like water, may the Great Gods pour it out! Like a goblet, may They dash it to pieces! Like a tile, may They break it!..."

MJ's voice was a comfort. A bright point amidst the mind-wrenching shriek, which was unending. It was more than merely an amelioration. MJ's litany spun outward into a thread of silver which grew, burgeoning into a shield which suspended above them. As it strengthened, it blossomed downward, bending into a convex dome.

The creature came forth. Clambering up, over the wreckage, over the small crest of embankment between Morris Boulevard and McKinley Avenue. It advanced perilously, leaching forward like living lava, which echoed a dissonance that was beyond pain.

It needed to be closer.

Taking in a breath, Nora launched into the spell to hold it. It needed to come across, to the park side. Yet it hovered there as if deciding whether to proceed. Nora did not wish to see the world from its perspective. It was deciding, but it should not resist the lure, the command of the Elder Tablet.

It's shriek crescendoed in an enfeebled attempt to countermand her. She could see the creature contract ever so slightly, but then it rebounded and tried splitting. It had decided. It would resist. Nora heard it in her mind. Her synapses scorched in its desire. It would try to take the Tablet, to gain mastery over itself—and its brethren lingering in their alien fourth-dimension. The dimension contained within the Tablet.

Nora nodded at MJ, who lit and tossed the first flare where it landed about an inch shy of where it needed to go. MJ lit another and another, tossing each at interval along the ring of Greek fire. They caught and so did the first. A ring of purple flames leapt forth, the exact shade as MJ's Volkswagen bus.

"It Shall Not Pass! May the Great Gods Entrap it! May the Great Gods Curse it! May the Great Gods Snare it! Should this barrier be tested....!

And it was upon them, enveloping the barrier with a sea of ophidian arabesques, littered with an oculary effervescence. At each point that it touched the dome, a necrosis danced across its surface.

Nora inhaled again and dispatched the unmaking.

The shriek dissolved into a burbling vociferation that melted into an absence of sound. There was a slight sucking, a pop, and the Tablet shuddered in Nora's hands.

The creature, the main creature was contained.

Nora fell to the ground in her exertion, clutching the Tablet to her chest. She began a prayer of thanks to her deities, chief amongst them Kali, who had helped them both in the past. "Om Sri Maha Kalikayai Namaha."

MJ bowed her head and took up the chant as the Greek fire continued to burn about them.

The women were left to their devotions for only a few moments. A wailing pierced the air and Nora thought that their efforts had been ineffectual. She felt the abyss open, but before she could despair, she realized the sound was a fire-engine headed toward them. She finished her last mantra and tucked the Tablet inside her jacket inside the waist of the front of her pants and zippered the light rain jacket she had been wearing over it.

Along with the firetrucks came a squadron of vehicles, mostly dark and unadorned, but several national guard vehicles. One pulled up right where the Shoggoth had been slavering mere moments before.

"Ladies. You've got to get out of here immediately. This area is being evacuated. It's under quarantine."

"What?" They both said simultaneously.

He was tall man, not unlike a Hugo Weaving. But of course, MJ thought, *had* to be Smith right? Doesn't the spook squad have anyone nice and friendly like Bilbo or Mr. Rogers? The guy wore black, with the requisite black tie. Thankfully nary a pair of sunglasses or neuralyzer in sight. Praise all the Goddesses.

"The Oyster Creek Power station has had a breach and we're evacuating the entire area until we can get it under control."

Nora and MJ were both kneeling by their camp table, a smoldering cauldron burning sweet herbs, amidst a smoking ring of burned matter that ate about half a foot down into the asphalt. The four houses between them and the water had been obliterated, along with half of Seaside Heights and more than a few areas between here and there.

Why did neither of them believe a nuclear meltdown was possible? And yet, the soldiers were knocking on doors and directing people to get in their vehicles and leave. Those who couldn't were being loaded onto what looked like a Vietnam era Deuce-and-a-half. Nora couldn't help but laugh. It was one of her father's favorite vehicles. When she was a girl, he had been an avid military-vehicle buff. She would recognize an M35 anywhere. He had owned two. One he named for her, much to her chagrin, at 10 years old.

MJ and Nora were escorted by "Mr. Smith" to the Volkswagen, where MJ had parked it on the far side of the park, at Morris, well away from the water.

"Professor Danforth, please contact my Director, Agent Mills, at your first opportunity. She needs to gather your account of this incident." "Mr. Smith" had put his hand on the driver's side door preventing either of the women from getting in.

"Doctor," Nora murmured.

"Excuse me?" The tall man stared at her as though she had more than a few protuberances.

"Dr. Danforth."

"My apologies." He handed her a card. "At your earliest convenience. An agent can be sent to your offices should you prefer that, *Doctor* Danforth."

"Yes, Agent—?"

"Call me Smith."

"Obviously. Agent Smith. Yes, please ask your Director Mills to have someone come to my office. I take it there is no nuclear risk?"

"That I don't know. I can't say."

"Ok. But after what we just went through? We won't be debriefed right now. We'll be getting our things and heading home."

"But there's an evacuation order."

"And we will evacuate. As soon as I get my things from the motel, which is a stone's throw from here. Then we will vacate. We expect to be back in Arkham in several days. Have Director Mills contact me for an appointment."

"But—"

"Here's *my* card." Nora pulled a card from her wallet, which she had tossed in the glove compartment. "Is it still Tuesday?"

"No, ma'am. It's actually Thursday, only just. But still Thursday."

"I never could get the hang of Thursdays. Have Director Mills or someone at my offices Monday if they'd rather not speak via phone, or make an appointment like normal folks."

As Agent Smith walked off wondering why this smallish,

white haired woman had the gall to tell him that his boss had to make an appointment, Nora climbed into the passenger seat.

"Too bad. Gilbert owes me a bottle of Patron. I'll collect, but after we rest up. You up for a drive home?"

"I think so. I'll take first shift?"

"Sure." Nora smiled wearily.

"Can I ask something? A few quick somethings?" MJ attempted a smile, but couldn't manage it. Her brain hurt. She started the van, feeling somewhat better in her father's old boat. She rolled up the windows. The smell of spent Greek fire turned her stomach. She realized she left Jaimie's cauldron on the camp table in the park. She'd get him a new one. He wasn't overly sentimental. She was not going back to that park or this neighborhood anytime soon.

Nora nodded.

"Was that all of them? There were *them*, right?"

"I hope that was. The accounts sounded like it might have reproduced."

"How? Without the Tablet, without an Elder Thing, *how*?"

"There are whole blogs dedicated to the reproduction of Shoggoths, MJ. My guess? Something in the atmosphere, in the water, something it was exposed to might have sparked a reaction."

"Sort of like daphnia? You remember from basic bio. When the water temperature is warm enough, daphnia self-replicate. The entire population is female. Clones of the original."

"Yes, but Shoggoth aren't exactly water fleas. And what was the factor? What caused the shift?"

"Fluorine."

"Huh?" Nora thought her assistant was reaching.

"Fluorine. The eruption of Mount Hekla. It's highly unusual... usually it's localized. See Hekla's tephra is very high in fluorine. It's in such concentrations that when there's an eruption, the fluorine contaminates the grasslands around the mountain, possibly the water as well, but I'm reaching there. It can kill grazing livestock. Farmers have to bring their animals inside and give them feed. And Hekla has been erupting for maybe a week now? It's one that can erupt for months, sometimes years. The dust cloud has already impacted air traffic. It cooled our temps. It started that rain, which looks like it's about ready to start up again any moment. So, why not consider that some of this fluorine has migrated here?"

"If that's the case, then that means the rain might be at higher acid levels. It's possible this evacuation isn't all fluff and nonsense. If there is a Hybrid cluster here, the rain might be affecting them. I'm going to have to speak with this Director Mills. See if there's anything more going on here. Acid rain and fish-frogs don't mix, MJ my dear. Let's get our gear."

"One more something, Nora."

Nora leaned her head back on the headrest. She couldn't argue. If it wasn't for MJ, for how strong she had become, then both of them would either not be here now or would have succumbed to some nightmarish Hybridization as the Shoggoth would have undoubtedly overwhelmed them. "Go ahead, MJ."

"Where is the creature now? It's not dead. That much is obvious. Had we expanded the Assyrian artillery— both the spell and the Greek Fire, perhaps, with enough effort, we cold have killed it. The Tablet... how does that work exactly?"

"I suppose," Nora closed her eyes a moment. Pulling at threads, joining them up. "I suppose the Tablet is not unlike Keziah Mason's gable room. It is a gateway to another dimension. But, one isolated from the rest of Euclidian and Einsteinian space-time. The Tablet opens a bifurcation in space. A portable worm-hole if, you will. It's like a quantum version of a djinn's lamp. So the Shoggoth was unmade in our realm and went back to what you can think of as a holding cell, hitherto one of those juxtapositions in space-time."

"Yeah...." MJ nodded. "So, yesterday's magic is today's science. I suppose there's more to the idea of witch-flight via broomstick. Since that's basically where Mason had travelled, I suppose. It's more than logical if you think about it....but, I can't think any more about it. Not now. Not until we need to write up our notes, file our reports. Let's drive for a bit? Get some breakfast. There's a wonderful little café over on 70. Amazing open-faced waffle sammiches. We can make a quick detour. Then any stops?"

"I think we might be able to make it to Champlins for lunch. My treat. I think I could demolish a few dozen oysters and a couple of nice stuffies."

"That sounds nice. Can I have mine now?"

They wanted to laugh, have a *Scooby Doo* end to this episode, but after seeing that thing? It would be some time before they laughed again.

MISKATONIC UNIVERSITY
SPECIAL COLLECTIONS DEPARTMENT
ITEM #973-C76
"ELDER TABLET"

Perhaps the strangest and most enigmatic piece in the Miskatonic University collection. This item, as told by an Innsmouth resident taken into custody during the "Innsmouth Raid of 1928", is said to come from an ancient pre-human race that once inhabited Antarctica. The tablet is said to contain instructions for creating a "Shoggoth," a creature told of in the Necronomicon of Alhazred. This item seems to correspond with reports of a large, unknown creature encountered by Bureau of Investigation agents in the sewers of Innsmouth during said raid. It is important to note that this piece has been stolen and recovered three separate times by vengeful Innsmouth residents since its initial seizure in 1928 and therefore not be loaned or examined by anyone other than Miskatonic University Special Collections Department staff.

EPILOGUE

Charlie was feeling much better. They were finally allowed to come back home, after spending more than two months in a hotel halfway across the state, almost in Pennsylvania. He thought it was funny. They had been staying maybe two hours away from Three Mile Island and he was sure about another half a dozen nuclear power stations.

He had no idea whether to believe any of what they had been told. But, at least they were home. His weather station had been destroyed. Along with most of Seaside Heights below Boulevard. But, they had all been here before. With Sandy. They rebuilt then. They'd do it again. Jersey Strong. Yup.

Mom was happy that their house hadn't been touched. She wasn't thrilled about the state of her checkered rug. But, at least they were all there. His feet were too. Dad didn't understand what he had been going on about, but then everything happened down the block and the boots were forgotten. Literally in the middle of mom's awful rug.

They were still there.

Mom and Dad were downstairs, tackling the horrors of a refrigerator with two months of rotting food in it. He thought Mom should've brought home some hazmat suits from that clean-up job she had been doing at the old Geigy site for like ever.

Charlie stood there in the middle of the sun room, staring at what he thought was a blob of fungus that had grown from his shoes and his old regurgitated ice cream.

Then the small blob, about the size and shape of a handball blinked at him. With one eye which blopped to the surface, blinked and popped like a soap-bubble.

“Are you my very own Mr. Ball-legs?” Charlie asked. “Or a baby demogorgon? I think if I had to choose, I'd choose Mr. Ball-legs. I'm not a big fan of all the antics of those demogorgon thingies.”

Again the eye-blink. “We can be whatever you wish, Charles.” A simpering, susurrus whispered into his mind. It felt nice. Lighter. His mind did. Although that weird scaly patch on the side of his neck had started itching again. Mom thought it was his eczema acting up. It was one of the reasons she never let him eat ice cream. Not really. She said it was a dairy allergy. But, his mind broadened. He felt almost giddy.

The creature itself lightened, too. It took on a light honey brown color. It reminded Charlie of his father's favorite brand of beer. Charlie had never had a pet. Well once. He had a toad. That didn't go well. He still had the habitat in his closet. He thought the glass was undamaged. He could clean it out pretty quickly.

“I think it would be nice to have a pet. Would you like to stay?”

“Yes. We would.”

“Sweet. I think I'll call you Honey Brown.”

FIN

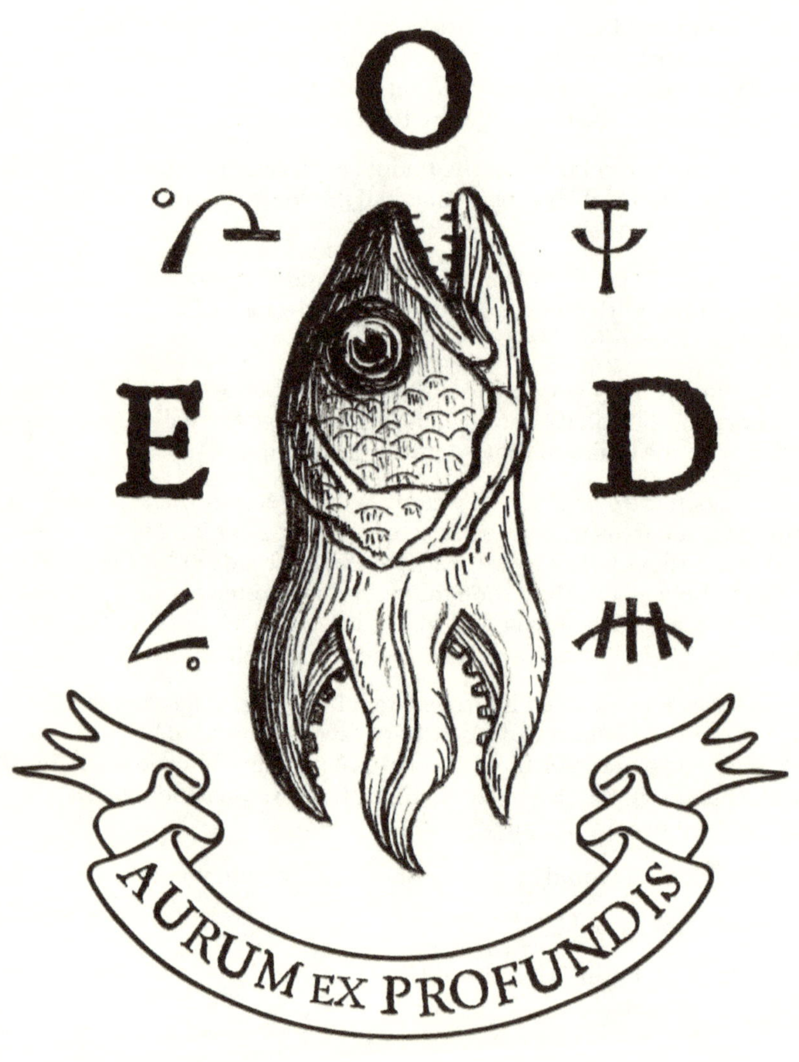

To get your own Elder Tablet visit
https://www.cryptocurium.com
https://www.etsy.com/shop/Cryptocurium
https://www.instagram.com/the_cryptocurium